Angel
Fever

Angel
Fever

Isobelle
Carmody

*This is for Richard Harland whose Ferren books
wakened my slumbering angel fever and for
Paul Collins who charmed and chivvied me
into Quentaris ...*

Thomas C. Lothian Pty Ltd
132 Albert Road, South Melbourne, Victoria 3205
www.lothian.com.au

Copyright © Isobelle Carmody 2004

First published 2004

National Library of Australia
Cataloguing-in-Publication data:

Carmody, Isobelle, 1958– .
Angel Fever

ISBN 0 7344 0689 4

1. Life on other planets — Juvenile fiction. 2. Quests (Expeditions) —
Juvenile fiction. 3. Magic — Juvenile fiction. I. Title.
(Series: Quentaris chronicles).

A823.3

Cover artwork by Marc McBride
Back cover artwork by Grant Gittus
Map by Jeremy Maitland-Smith
Original map by Marc McBride
Cover and text design by John van Loon
Printed in Australia by Griffin Press

Contents

QUEN

ARIS

A
Cry
for Help

It was a mean day full of stinging rain and blustery winds that slapped from all directions. Eely clung tightly to her cloak, knowing that Cora would be angry if it flew away. She was anxious to do nothing that would trouble or upset her older sister because Cora was trying to decide whether or not to accept a promotion to captain in the army. Eely was almost as much afraid that Cora would refuse it as that she would accept. Because if she refused, it would be Eely's fault.

The trouble was that if Cora became captain, she would have to move into the barracks. Everyone assigned rift duty was supposed to live there, but until now Cora had been permitted to live away from the barracks with Eely so long as she was not late for parade and did not miss an inspection. That had never been a problem because Cora was the sort of person you could rely on to be responsible when it came to rules. Even when they were both small and Cora had made up the rules to the games they played, she had insisted they obey them even if it meant that she would lose.

If only things didn't have to change, Eely thought. But then she remembered her sister's round, glowing face and the pride in her eyes and felt ashamed of her selfishness. Because of course

Cora deserved to be promoted. She was thorough and responsible and good at making people do the right thing without ever shouting or getting angry. She was everything a good captain should be. And why not? In a way, she had been captain of Eely since their parents had been killed during one of the regular outbreaks between the two feuding families in Quentaris, the Greens and Blues, years ago.

She ignored the icy trickle of rainwater down her neck, telling herself that she ought to be glad that the weather was horrible since it meant the urchins who currently claimed the Square of the People as their territory were at home keeping warm instead of pelting her with mud balls. The square was almost deserted as she hurried across it. There was just one of the Dung Brigade miserably scraping at the cobbles, his bucket beside him, and two Greens striding in the opposite direction, deep in conversation.

Eely had to lean into the wind to make any headway because it was stronger in the open, and she was glad to reach the other side and turn onto the street that led towards the Last and First Station. The wind was less fierce here and if she kept close to the walls of the buildings, she could even get out of the rain.

The lunch pail was heavy because she had got soup from the Paupers' market, and she switched it to the other hand, slowing down because she was early. Eely was supposed to arrive exactly at the beginning of the noon meal break, so that Cora would just have finished her shift, and normally she arrived right on time. But today Ma Coglin had insisted she leave early because she had started early, refusing to listen when Eely said she liked helping out in the soup kitchen.

Of course she couldn't tell that to Cora, who disapproved of the Paupers' market because she said that it was a hotbed of strife where escaped slaves and other troublemakers met to hatch plots. Ma Coglin had warned Eely that no one official liked the Paupers' market since a barter market could not be taxed. The soup kitchen was not really anything to do with the market except that at the end of the day, leftover food from stalls was traditionally given to

it. But most of the food offered free at the soup
kitchen had been cadged and begged and guilted out
of the big rich houses and eating establishments in
Quentaris by the formidable Ma Coglin. Eely liked
helping and she liked Ma Coglin, but she had got in
the habit of saying nothing about her time there
because she did not want to annoy Cora.

Eely's thoughts swung back to the present as she
passed the imposing triple entrance to the rift house
and she slanted a shy look of longing towards it, half
hoping to see one of the senior guides coming out. In
her secret dreams Eely was a fearless rift guide
leading people into the many-faceted darkness of the
caves that riddled the cliffs looming over the city.

She could never really be a guide of course, any
more than she could be a rift guard. She was not
physically strong or brave as rift guards and guides
always were. Most of all she wasn't *smart*. Not like
Mama and Papa had been. Not even smart in the
practical way that Cora was smart. Something had
gone wrong when Eely was being born and it had
taken too long for her to come out. Eely's mind had
been hurt by the waiting, Mama had explained once

to her. Eely always imagined that something had slipped out of her when she was inside Mama in the darkness waiting to be born, and that this bit of her had lost its way. Sometimes she imagined it was still lost somewhere, that missing bit, waiting for her to find it.

It was not until she came to the entrance to the Last and First Station that she could see the rift wall which separated the long low guardroom and its adjacent gatehouse from the stony stretch of open ground that led up to the rift caves. Out of habit, Eely made sure not to look behind her at the Undertakers' Guild house. Most of the undertaker novices ignored her but there were two bigger girls that sometimes sat out on the steps, who would taunt her and call her a dummy. They never threw things as the urchins did, but their words hurt worse than any mud ball. They fell inside her like great hard stones, and sometimes she imagined that she was so full of those stone words that if she went into the water, she would sink straight to the bottom.

'Hey Eely,' a voice called from the tiny box that was the gatehouse.

Eely smiled because the voice belonged to the big craggy-looking rift guard, Red, who was one of the few people who ever remembered her name. Probably it was because of Cora being his friend, but Eely was always glad to find he was on the gate. None of the other guards were unkind or cruel, but Eely hated the way most of them looked through her when they spoke to her. Sometimes when they did that, she had the creepy feeling that she was fading away. The truth was that she preferred the two nasty undertaker novices and the tormenting urchins because at least they saw her.

'Are you well, Eely?' Red asked gently, and she flushed because she had done it again. Gone off into her own thoughts right in the middle of trying to talk to someone.

'I … I'm fine, sir,' she stammered.

'Red,' Red said, as he always did, smiling so that the edges of his eyes crinkled up. 'But I have some bad news for you, Eely. Cora will be late today. We're having trouble with a flock of harpies that came through a rift last night. She's gone into the caves with a couple of guides and most of the other guards to try and round them up and drive them back where they belong. They'll cause havoc if they escape into the city.' He glanced up at the black sky. 'Why don't you go to the barracks and wait? There's a nice fire there and you can dry out.'

'Can't I wait here?' Eely asked quickly.

Red gave her a searching look that made her feel he was looking inside her head and seeing her secret thoughts. 'Are you sure you are all right?'

'Yes. I … I am, really,' Eely said. 'Can I wait here for Cora?'

'Of course you can, but …' He glanced up into the sky. 'I don't think the rain is going to let up any time soon and the guardroom is locked because one of the others has the key. Maybe you should go round and sit on the other side of the rift wall? At least you'll have a bit of shelter from the rain there.'

Eely nodded and slipped away through the gate with relief. She liked Red but she never seemed to be able to just talk normally to him. She always stammered and said idiotic things. She sat with her back to the stone wall and stared at the cliffs, which grew less and less visible as the rain fell in a slanting grey curtain, the drumming sound of it drowning out all other noise. If she squinted, Eely could just make out the nearer caves.

≥

She was daydreaming that she was a great rift guard in the caves and had just discovered an incredible treasure, when a movement across the sodden open ground caught her attention. She squinted and saw that a rift guard had come out of the farthest cave. He was shouting and gesticulating towards the gatehouse, but it was raining too hard to make his words out. Red ran over to join him and after a moment of conversation, they both suddenly turned and disappeared into the cave!

Red had forgotten about her, of course, and Eely wasn't offended because people often forgot her. But she was surprised that he had left the gate unmanned because someone was always supposed to be there. She thought he would come back out of the cave almost at once, but when he didn't, a thought so strange and daring came to Eely that she began to tremble.

What if she walked over to the rift cave and entered it?

It was a thought so unusual to her that Eely wondered if it hadn't come because of Cora having to decide about being a captain. Because if she could go into a rift cave, perhaps she would find a way to be brave enough to let Cora be free of her.

Eely had never thought of herself as a burden before but her heart grew heavy at the knowledge that it was true. She *was* a burden to Cora; a slow-witted little sister, too frightened and silly to look after herself.

Much too quickly, Eely was standing before a rift cave, her heart banging so hard in her chest that it was making her feel sick. Her momentary bravado trickled away as fast as water spilled in soft sand and she knew that she could not possibly enter the rift cave. She must have gone mad for a second to imagine she could.

She had taken one step back when she heard a faint cry from within the cave.

'Help … me …' a voice called. A man's voice, weak and breathy as if he were hurt. And frightened. It was the fear that caught at Eely. Because she knew what it was to be frightened and to call for help. She knew how terrible it was when no one came, and how wonderfully like a miracle it was when someone did.

But Eely was frightened, too, and she had never done anything to defy the voice of fear in her mind. That voice now reminded her that the rift caves were dangerous. It pointed out that slavers sometimes ventured through the rifts from other worlds, or monsters of various kinds. The caves were full of danger, even before you got to the rift parts; poisonous vapours would ooze from chasms opened up by unexpected shudders and shifts in the unstable ground. These were some of the reasons that the rift caves were guarded, and why adventurers wanting to enter them had to register themselves with the rift guards.

But someone needed help and Ma Coglin always said helping people was something everyone ought to do, if they could. She licked her lips and thought of running to the barracks for help. But by the time she managed to find someone and get them to listen to her, it could very well be too late. Maybe it was too late already.

Eely was entering the cave even before she realised that she had decided to go in. It was very dark inside and air seemed to flow outward, though how that could be possible, she couldn't imagine. Unless it was true, as she had once dreamed, that there was a great storm at the heart of the rift caves.

She heard the cry again, fainter than before, and groped her way towards the voice. The cold wind brushing her cheeks smelled of wet clay and something faintly sulfurous, like an egg gone bad. Somewhere, Eely could hear the sound of water trickling and there was a rustling in the darkness that she told herself was a bat. Just a bat. Everyone knew the rift caves were full of them.

Then she saw a faint light ahead.

It was coming out of a cave which ran off from the tunnel that she was in and Eely approached its entrance warily. Her mouth dropped open in shock when she saw inside, for right in the centre of the cave, black hair draggling down its filthy back between two black leathery wings, was a *harpy*!

Eely nearly fainted out of terror, for she knew that one slash of its claws would poison her blood and no healer in all Quentaris could save her from the screaming madness that would follow. The voice of fear gibbered at her to get back, get away, run, but paradoxically her fear was so great that it paralysed her. So she saw the harpy hop sideways on its claws and tilt its head down to look at its victim. Eely realised that this must be the poor man who had called out, only she was too late, for he was dead. Full of remorse, Eely prepared herself to back away quietly when the harpy shifted again and she saw the man lying on the ground properly.

The first thing she noticed was that he was the source of pale white light illuminating the harpy and the cave. The second thing she noticed was that despite being bloodied and battered, the man was handsome enough to almost take her breath away.

The third thing she noticed *did* take her breath away, for the shining man had great soft white wings. There had been winged exotics visiting Quentaris of course, but they had not been like this man. He was so handsome and pale and perfect and his wings were so white and pure where they had not been broken and besmirched. It came to Eely with dawning wonder that he was not human at all, but one of those beings that Mama had always said watched over people like her. Angels, she called them, because that was what her mother called them, when she told Mama the story of the wondrous beings whose magic came from their purity and goodness. Eely had believed passionately in angels when she was little, but she had stopped believing when she got older, because if such a being watched over her, why hadn't it stopped people hurting her?

Now, seeing the angel, she wondered if only

people who were especially worthy got angels to look after them. Or, since angels knew everything, maybe her guardian angel had known that she would stop believing in it, and so it had fled from her lack of faith.

'No!' the angel moaned suddenly, tossing its golden head. The harpy gave a hiss of alarm and flapped a few feet away. Then it moved towards the angel again, lifting one of its vicious talons decisively.

'Oh don't!' screamed Eely, stumbling forward half dazed with the intensity of her longing.

The harpy turned at once, and gave a dreadful shrieking scream that seemed to rend the air. Eely cringed in pain and the harpy leapt at her. Without thought, Eely swung up the heavy lunch pail and by chance or luck, it hit the harpy a great thudding blow under her pointed chin. She fell like a rock and lay motionless at Eely's feet.

In dismay and trembling from head to toe, Eely stared down at the creature, suddenly seeing how very old and frail-looking the harpy was without its fury. The thought that she had killed it made Eely bend over and vomit her breakfast onto the ground. Only when she had retched and heaved until her stomach ached did she gather her wits and edge past the harpy to go to the angel. He was almost twice the height of an ordinary man, yet for all his size, he was perfectly proportioned. His hair was short and so soft that it shifted under her breath, but it was his wings that demanded her gaze. They were exactly like a dove's wings, but many, many times larger and perfectly, luminously white. The smallest of the feathers in them were as long as her arm and a passionate desire came over Eely to touch those wings. She reached out only to snatch her hand back guiltily when the angel stirred.

She dared a glance at his face and was relieved to find his eyes were still shut fast. She had the muddled idea that it might be forbidden to look into the face of an angel, especially one who was uncon-scious and vulnerable. But now that she had looked, she could not look away. She found herself studying each of the angel's features apart from the rest, because to look at his whole face was to be half stunned.

His nose, for instance, seemed to her a little sculpture of perfection that she could look at for hours, while his thick, gold-tipped eyelashes lay curled delicately against the smooth curve of his cheeks, making her long to see the eyes that lay behind them. His skin was velvety and pale as the innermost petals of a white rose. The one thing that seemed out of place was his mouth, which was not at all the sort of mouth Eely would have imagined for an angel. His lips were very full and stained red as if he had been eating fresh cherries.

The
Cloudlands

Nonaerom walked lightly along the lane towards the city centre, his mind occupied more with thoughts of the wingstone than with the street about him.

But eventually the unrelenting sameness of the dingy building facades demanded his unwilling attention. He disliked Landfall City, as did all of the wingborn, though their own ancestors had helped to build it and had once dwelt here. Back in those days, there had been free and frequent breeding between the winged and wingless, though it was considered bad taste to refer directly to it these days. The influential younger royalty now counted their importance by how long it had been since the pure blood of their line had mingled with that of a land walker. The fact that his own great grandmother had joined to a land walker, even after most of the winged had gone to dwell in the newly constructed Cloud City, was a source of shame to him. No one mentioned it outright, of course, but Nonaerom knew that the stigma had harmed him more than once when it came to important moments in his life. Even now when it was openly accepted that he would succeed as king of the Cloudlands, he felt his great grandmother's mistake fuelled a subtle opposition to his taking the throne. And when the suggestion had come that the king might retire, the king had not disputed the idea, but it had not come to pass.

Nonaerom might have suspected that the king himself had reservations about the prince to whom he had previously shown such great favour, except that the king had frankly told Nonaerom he looked forward to retiring and wished to do so before another turn of the seasons.

'Unfortunately the wingstone is proving increasingly elusive and it is being whispered that it is displeased with the wingborn, or that it has wearied of our attempts to produce a beauty potent enough to satisfy its hunger.' The king's eyes flashed with humour. 'Of course, some of my counsellors suggest gently and others not so gently, that the wingstone tires of me. But I have not changed, nor has my devotion to beauty. Indeed I would retire only so as to have time to follow my own artistic desires and produce objects which would be worthy of the stone's hunger. I think it is some other thing that ails it, but I doubt we can easily learn the nature of that trouble, for the wingstone is a thing utterly different from us and our kind. It is a mystery and a miracle bestowed upon us by chance and if we are to learn more of it, I think it will demand devoted study for many hundreds of years. I have dreamed that it will be your task to learn more of the wingstone. The thing is to ensure that you will have that time. If I abdicate now as I desire to do, you will inherit both the troubled nature of the wingstone and the rumour that it was discontented with my rule and with my choice of a successor. If such a rumour were to gain strength it would destabilise the Cloudlands, and I cannot allow that to happen.'

'What would you have me do, my king? Should I quest to discover what troubles the wingstone?' Nonaerom had asked gracefully, ensuring that his tone was pleasingly modulated between deference and firmness, and that neither dismay nor furious pride showed in his words.

The king had given him a quick bright knowing glance that told Nonaerom the older man knew exactly what response his words had ignited. But rather than chiding him for his lack of subtlety, the king said with shocking simplicity, 'I think you will make a good king, my son. But before you take the throne, you had better show that you can hold the wingstone. Therefore I have decided that you will be the bearer of the wingstone for this season, in anticipation and in trust for when you will hold it as ruler of the Cloudlands. Keep it with you and do not let it slip away until this season ends and none will have the gall to suggest that you are not worthy.'

Nonaerom had flinched at that, because it was unpardonably blunt and in the Cloudlands, blunt equated with ugly. Ugliness had no place among the winged folk for it wounded the wingstone and therefore the magic that held the lovely city aloft. In ordinary circumstances, to say something too simply was to admit oneself a simpleton.

But the king was neither simpleton nor fool. And he was right. Nonaerom drew himself up to his full height, and he was tall among the winged folk.

'Your trust honours me,' he told the king, meaning it.

The trouble was that bearing the wingstone was a far more difficult task than anyone would have imagined, for it had ways of slipping from a hand or rolling into a difficult corner or easing its way out of a pocket. The only safe way to keep it was, Nonaerom had finally decided, to literally hold it in his hand all of the time, and that was what he did. He held it and tried always to be aware of holding it, because the stone became active when he least expected it. It was hard to think an object that he had spent his life revering and longing for was an opportunist, but Nonaerom had come to find the wingstone sly and clever and he never let it out of his hand or mind for a moment.

Even so, there had been a few close calls in the beginning, when he had almost lost it. He had managed to get it back before it could disappear completely, but that had been when he had formed the idea that the phrase *Holding the wingstone* could have a literal interpretation.

Thus had he managed to bear it safely for half a season, but the effort was beginning to tell. He constantly felt anxious and uneasy, and rather than slipping from his mind, these days the wingstone seemed to loom in his mind in a way that was almost sinister.

He shook his head and told himself not to be foolish. He had only a few sevendays to go, and then the king would step down and he would take the throne. Of course, doing that meant accepting responsibility for the wingstone for several hundred years, but he was prepared for that now, and he had some thoughts about how it might be more comfortably done. His first task as king would to be commission a great inquiry with many scholars and philosophers who would investigate the nature of the wingstone, and seek to understand what it was and how it worked and, most of all, what troubled it and made it so difficult to hold.

His mind was so much on his own problems that he hardly looked about him, so he did not see a group of young men watching him from a sidewalk, their eyes hot and sullen.

'Featherbrain.'

Nonaerom looked around in outrage and saw a group of young land walkers sitting on the steps of the building just ahead.

'What did you say?' he asked, giving them a cold stare.

One of the group uncoiled in a lithe movement that Nonaerom could not help but appreciate. 'I said Featherbrain, but on second thoughts, I prefer Chicken-hawk.'

Nonaerom felt surprise before anger, for land walkers so seldom dared offer aggression to winged folk because of their superior size and strength. That surprise made him slow to react when one of the young men moved to hurl a stone. It glanced off his shoulder and Nonaerom's anger began to unfurl along with his wings. These mud slugs would pay if they had scarred his arm! Without warning, two more of the group threw a small but efficient snare net that, although it did not contain him, stopped Nonaerom unfolding his wings properly. In a moment, shockingly, the land walkers were upon him, their combined weight bearing him down.

Nonaerom, stunned and disbelieving that land walkers would handle a winged prince in this rough way, was borne down to the ground under their combined weight, and his face pressed into the dirt!

Dirt!

'Taste it, you winged freak!' One of the men screamed. It was the bitter hatred in his words more than their meaning, that caused fear to writhe in Nonaerom's belly, but then the sense of the words sank in, too.

Freak! He had heard gossip that the land walkers were beginning to call those with wings freaks, but he had dismissed it, for how could anyone, even a dull-witted mud slug, see wings as anything but things of beauty and grace? It was a signal of their decline that they would dare to think thus of winged folk whose lives were dedicated to beauty. The land walkers had become all but beasts.

He did not struggle, and that seemed to anger the men more. One of them hit him and suddenly blows were raining down painfully. He saw his own blood soaking into the dark and hungry earth, but he could not bring himself to offer the grace of his words to these grunting beasts. So they seemed to him, and their fury seemed to grow rather than to spend itself in their orgy of violence.

That was when he felt someone take hold of his wing and draw it out. He turned to see a young woman, her eyes slitted and vicious. 'Let's bring him down to earth,' she hissed, making a motion. Before Nonaerom could begin to realise what she intended, two men rose and began to stamp on the wing, breaking it, grinding it into the dirt. He heard the delicate bones snapping. Blood flowed until the wing was no longer white but brown and crusted with filth. Broken!

He gave a cry of anguish more than pain, for that was like a distant cloud heralding an approaching storm. Then one of the other men began to kick him and Nonaerom realised with a dreaming, swooning terror, that they meant to kill him.

'Wait!'

It was the woman again. Nonaerom saw her through one swollen eye. The other was a haze of red fire embedded in his face and he kept it closed lest movement fan the flames of agony waiting to blaze there.

'I want to kill him,' the woman said. 'Him and all of his kind for turning us into slaves. "Mud slugs" they call us. Dirt eaters who work as slaves to serve them in their city in the clouds. Why should I give them my hard earned grain, or Olec his weaves? Why shouldn't they offer trade goods instead of taking and taking?'

'We give … you beauty …' Nonaerom managed to say through split lips, feeling the horrible sharpness of broken teeth under his tongue.

A man snarled at him like a rabid wolf, his face contorted with savagery. 'I don't care about beauty. My children and I must slave and struggle to serve you. There is no beauty in slavery.' He lifted his great hammer of a fist, but again the woman stopped him.

She was still kneeling in a mockery of reverence beside the savaged wing, one hand outstretched to halt the actions of the men. Was it mercy or some mote of pity or regret that moved her?

'Wait. I have changed my mind. Death will be too quick. Let us throw him into the Aurora vortex. They say eternity lies at the heart of it, and I want him to suffer forever. Him and all his kind.' She pushed a face that might have been beautiful if it had not been contorted with rage, into Nonaerom's face. 'But do not fear. It will not be long before you have company, winged man, for we will send all your folk screaming into the vortex, their wings and faces smashed and bloodied.'

He tried to speak then. To offer the eloquence that, even more than his great beauty and physical grace, had won him his place as leader of the winged royals. He might have convinced them, for they were only land walkers and his words would give their hearts wings so that they would understand and be appalled at what they had done. But his mouth was too bruised and he could not gather his wits and serenity to formulate the words before they were lifting him roughly between them, grunting at the size of him. Then they were carrying him, cursing his weight, and he could not speak because the storm of pain had arrived and was roaring through him.

He fainted and then woke and fainted again to their panting as they heaved him over the rocks towards the strange phenomenon of distorting air called the Aurora vortex. The very place where, some said, the first winged man had found the wing-stone which had, aside from becoming the symbol of rulership of the winged folk, held the Cloudlands aloft.

Then Nonaerom remembered with horror that *he* was bearer of the wingstone. *Literally!* The only reason that he had not dropped it while he was being beaten was because he had so rigorously trained himself never to relax his grip.

And if they threw him into the vortex, he would take the precious wingstone with him to oblivion. It would be lost to the winged folk and it was said if that came to pass, they would fall from grace. All of them, forever.

'No! You must not! I am the bearer of ...' he

mumbled, trying to struggle, but all the bones in him were limp and would not respond to his will.

'*Must not!*' The woman mocked him fiercely. 'It is the end of your kind saying *Must* or *Must not* to us!'

She nodded a command and Nonaerom was flying up. He tried to let go of the wingstone, so that at least it should remain in the world and with it, the possibility, however small, that it would be found and restored to its rightful holder, but his hand would not open. Then he entered the wavering, whirling Aurora vortex and light seemed to pierce him at once from all directions. He felt himself filled up with it, swelling and bloating, and then he was splitting open and the light was flying out of him, and he was falling in a thousand pieces; a coruscating blizzard of pain and blood and bitterest regret.

He woke what seemed eons later, the bones of the earth gouging into his back, but he could not move to ease himself for pain sat heavily on every limb and feasted. Yet he was *somewhere*, despite having been cast into the Aurora vortex, and despite everything, a flicker of curiosity woke his will. He forced open the one eye that would respond and saw the hideous face of all nightmares gazing down at him. It was a woman, but the foulest corruption of womanhood possible. Its eyes were blood red and hungry, and instead of a mouth, it had a beak rimmed with blackened teeth.

'Are we properly dead? Are we tasty yet?' The words came to him in a cloud of stench that would have made him scream and plead to escape, if he had been capable of speech. She leaned closer and the reek of her was so unbearable that he found his voice.

'No! Stay away from me!' he croaked. 'You will harm the wingstone. It cannot abide ugliness ...'

But still she came, and he closed his eyes and sank into the painless dark.

~

When he floated again to the surface of his mind, he opened his eyes and found a young woman was looking down at him. A transcendent vision of beauty so profound than he thought he must be dead, for she was above and beyond all things.

'Angel ...' he whispered, and being impossibly balanced between bliss and agony, he did the only thing he could do.

He fainted.

3

A
Fallen
Angel

Eely ran out of the rift cave only to cannon into Red's very firm chest. He caught hold of her shoulders to steady her and she felt a surge of relief, until she saw that he was looking at her with stern surprise and disapproval. She wondered if he had so completely forgotten her that he didn't even remember telling her that she ought to go through the gate and wait out of the rain.

'Where is my brother?' he demanded.

Eely goggled at him stupidly, and he gave her a little shake. 'Answer me girl. Where is the rift guard, Red? He was supposed to be on gate duty today.'

'Har … harpies,' Eely managed to say, trying to understand why Red would be asking about himself in this strange way.

He growled in his throat exactly as he always did when something troubled him. 'Look. I am Red's twin brother, Igorik. I had the feeling he needed me so I came, but perhaps it was only …' He stopped, letting go of Eely and shaking his head in exasperation. He ran blunt fingers through his red hair and since this was something that Red never did, it allowed Eely to see that, after all, this was not Red. She now noticed, too, that he wore the brown armband of a drainer.

'I … I didn't know he had a twin,' she managed to say.

Red's brother gave Red's shrug. Then he looked at Eely properly, and it gave her a little jolt to discover that, like his brother, he *saw* her as most Quentarans did not. 'What are you doing in here anyway?' he demanded.

'Red said I could wait out of the rain,' Eely said hurriedly.

'My brother told you to wait in a rift cave?' Red's brother lifted his red brows.

But his disbelief made no impact, for Eely gave a gasp, remembering all at once why she had gone into the cave. Incredible to think that she could have forgotten about the angel; as if finding him was an ordinary event that could be forgotten!

'Oh please! You have to help me. I wouldn't have gone in but I heard someone calling out and there was no gate guard so I ...'

'Someone is hurt?'

Eely's anxiety was so great that she caught the man by his great strong arm and simply tugged him towards the cave. He could easily have resisted, but he allowed her to draw him into the rift cave, his eyes adjusting quickly to the darkness. Like most drain dwellers, he had paid to have his eyes magically augmented, so he spotted the glow from the opening some way into the tunnel long before Eely could discern it. But her memory was clearly vivid enough for she made her way towards it unerringly. Suddenly she began talking, explaining about following the weak cries into the cave. When she came to the part of her story where the harpy was crouching over someone lying on the ground, Igorik stopped. 'A harpy! We will need special nets if we are to tangle with such a creature.'

'No! No, please come. She's dead. I killed her.' They had got close enough to the glow for Eely to see the look on his face, which she misread as horror at what she had done. She gave a little sob of anguish. 'It was an accident! I didn't mean to hurt her but she was going to hurt him and I cried out to her to stop so she flew at me. I hit her with my lunch pail because I was frightened ...'

'You hit a harpy on the head with your lunch pail,' Igorik said flatly.

'On the chin,' Eely said. 'See?'

They had reached the opening of the cave and she

stepped aside to let Igorik see into it properly. He stared at the harpy lying in a ragged black huddle in the centre of the cave, knowing it was impossible that this slight child could have immobilised a harpy and yet unable to doubt the sincerity in her simple, earnest expression. Of course the harpy was not dead. It took a good deal more than a blow from a lunch pail, however heavy, to stop a harpy, let alone kill one. It was probably stunned. But still, to render a harpy unconscious …

'Where is the man she hurt?' he asked, thinking they had better be out of the cavern before the harpy regained her malevolent senses.

'He … He's not a man,' Eely said in a peculiar voice. 'He … He's over here.'

Igorik followed her, and was startled to see that the faint light within the cavern which he had thought must emanate from a fungus, came from the form of a man. Then he saw, as Eely had, that it was no ordinary man.

'It is an angel,' Eely said breathlessly, and that was startling enough that Igorik managed to tear his fascinated gaze from the winged man, for angels were imaginary beings from a tale brought to Quentaris by a traveller when he was a boy. But Eely's expression glowed with such awe and joy that he had not the heart to tell her there were no such things.

So he merely nodded and moved closer to the winged man, taking in the appalling state of one wing. It lay stretched out at such an awkward angle that it must be broken. The edges were so torn that it looked as if they had been passed through a washing mangle with teeth. It might have been the work of one of the monsters that dwelt in the world beyond the rift, but for the clear bloody imprints of boots several times larger than his own.

Instinctively, he glanced down at the feet of the winged man, but he wore the lightest sandals and his feet did not look as if they were ever encased in more. Igorik turned his eyes back to the wing and thought that whoever had done this had not acted in mindless rage. There was an intensity and focus in the harm that had been done, for although the winged man's face and chest and arms were bloodied and battered, the worst hurt had been done to the wing. Deliberately.

That anyone could be capable of such viciousness sickened Igorik despite his pessimistic nature, but none of these thoughts showed on his face, for he sensed they would frighten Eely.

'I ... I think he might be hurt inside,' Eely said. Only then did Igorik notice that the winged man was gasping like a landed fish drowning on air. Closer inspection revealed that there was no fresh blood on his lips to indicate internal injuries and after listening a moment longer to the unconscious man's breathing, he wondered if it might not simply be the Quentaran air troubling him. Occasionally those who came through the rifts discovered the air was slightly wrong for them and they had some difficulty until they adjusted to it. But he had never heard of a visitor finding the air completely lethal. The possibility of different air might also mean that other aspects of the winged man's world differed, thereby explaining the scale of his form and the glow of his wings.

'Can you help him?' Eely begged.

Igorik nodded. 'We ought to get him out, but I'm afraid I could not manage him alone. I will go and get some of the other guards.'

'I will wait here,' Eely said, her eyes returning to the winged giant. She crossed her legs and sat by his head with the dogged air of a faithful drain hound.

Igorik glanced at the unmoving form of the harpy and decided it would only take a few minutes to round up some of the guards and return, and he would be quicker alone. 'All right. I will be back soon.'

≥

Eely did not look up as he hastened out. She was glad to be alone with the angel again, for she realised that quite soon he would be taken from her. She was not regretful because in Eely's life, little had belonged to her that she cherished, except when the things she desired were wanted by no one else.

She feasted her eyes on the angel's beauty, wondering what it would be to see him fly. She thought perhaps that sight might be at the heart of all she could ever desire. But after a little while, she found herself looking at his lips again and the strange vividness of them. They were hurt and swollen on one side, but even the unhurt part of them was very red. She could almost imagine that his mouth would be sticky and sweet to the taste.

'No! You must not! I am the Holder of ...'

Eely almost jumped out of her skin when the mouth she had been studying so closely moved. She lifted her gaze and found the angel's eyes open. They were a piercing, impossible blue and full of accusation. Eely quailed at the thought of having provoked their outrage, but then she saw that the angel was not really looking at her. She felt a moment of sickening disappointment that even an angel would not see her, but then the angel moaned and lifted one bloodied hand as if to ward off a blow, and Eely understood that he was not seeing *anything*.

'No! Stay away from me! You will harm the ...' His voice trailed off and then, without warning, he threw up his hand. It struck the cave wall behind him and something flew in a glittering arc from his fingers into Eely's lap.

It was a feather carved from glass or crystal, as long as Eely's longest finger. It was a perfect copy of a real feather in the tiniest detail, each single strand separately carved. She could not imagine how any artisan could manage such a thing. Perhaps it was not a carving, but the feather of a crystal bird. Such things might dwell where angels flew.

She held it up and the feather caught the dim glow of the angel, magnifying it so strongly that it filled the cave with a myriad of shivering light darts.

The angel moaned again and Eely slipped the carving into her pocket, then lay a hand on his shoulder to try to draw him from his nightmare.

At her touch, the angel's gaze immediately sharpened and now he *did* see her. Such was the will behind his gaze that Eely felt mesmerised. Never had she been *seen* so deeply. Something in Eely which had hitherto been as vague as smoke, seemed to take shape in her breast, but there was no time to wonder at it.

'Angel,' he whispered suddenly, and the word

echoed about them in the cave, filling the air with the sound of wings. Then his eyes fell closed and the loss of his marvellous confirming regard was so great that now it was Eely who cried out.

'Eely!'

Eely turned to find Red running across the cave towards her. His expression of concern told her that he really was Red, but it was still a little shock to see his brother coming along behind him, like enough to be a mirror copy of him.

'Are you hurt?' Red asked, kneeling by her, then his voice tailed off as he saw the winged man. 'Incredible,' he muttered. 'That wing …'

'Come on, before the harpy wakes up,' Igorik said impatiently, and Eely stood back to let the two men heave the angel up between them. Standing upright, he would have towered over them, so even when they had his arms hooked around their shoulders, he sagged to his knees. They managed to get him past the harpy, which was indeed beginning to stir, but they had to put him down again in the tunnel, because he was too heavy.

Fortunately, just at that moment some of the other guards came running in behind Cora. She commanded several of them to attend to the harpy while the rest were assigned to help Red and Igorik carry the winged man out of the cave. It was raining again as they bore him to the guard room, which was now open, and the angel was soaked through by the time they lay him on the long table that was the central piece in the big spartan room. One of the guards lay a dry cloak over him, avoiding the injured wing which looked worse than ever in the light flowing through the windows.

'He needs treatment, but I can't afford enough guards to carry him all the way across town to the Orphans' Hospital,' Cora said in her usual decisive way.

'I could take him to my den and get a physician to come and see him,' Igorik said. 'But it would be difficult and probably painful for him to be carried down into the drains.'

'We could have him at our house,' Eely said eagerly.

Cora frowned. 'It's too far, Eely, and where would we put him anyway? Besides, he needs to be with people capable of looking after him.'

Eely flinched and though Cora did not see, Red did. 'Steady on, Cora,' he said. 'Eely managed to defend him from a harpy well enough.'

'Knocking out the harpy was a pure accident. Eely is not capable of taking care of herself, let alone an injured man.'

Such bluntness would normally have silenced Eely for days, but she was too worried about the angel. 'Cora, maybe they could carry him to the Soothsayers' Guild house,' she persisted. 'There is a roost on their roof.'

'That's a good idea,' Igorik said. 'He has wings so the roofies will certainly agree to take him.'

'All right,' Cora said distractedly. 'Red, you and the others get him there as fast as you can and return at once. I need you in the caves.'

Igorik nodded to Eely. 'Run ahead and tell them we're coming, girl. We'll need help getting him up and I don't want to stand around arguing with people who think anyone whose feet touch the ground are tainted.'

Eely nodded, her heart pounding with the importance of her role.

⚊

They were soon hurrying through the streets, Eely trotting ahead of Igorik and the rift guards, her shoulders hunched against the rain.

'So what were you doing at the rift caves, anyway?' Red asked his twin.

Igorik sighed. 'Had the feeling you needed me, of course. I was up and running before I knew what I was doing. Then I thought I might as well come by, because it might be like all the other times, but maybe not. Then that child cannoned into me babbling about angels.'

'Angels?' Red asked, lowering his voice. 'But they're only a story.'

'Even so, your Eely thinks the winged man is an angel,' Igorik said.

'Well, whatever he is, he inspired some pretty devilish thoughts in someone.'

'In a few someones, I'd say,' Igorik murmured, then he fell silent, concentrating on bearing the weight of the winged man.

The
Roofies

'I don't care what Arrow thinks,' Iakas snapped. The truth was that she was heartily sick of hearing the lofty pronouncements of Arrow's devotees. And maybe that was why she had conceived of setting herself against the would-be leader of the roofies.

'You need not snarl at me,' Owl said in a wounded voice. She turned and made her way gracefully over the ornate ridge line of the Soothsayers' Guild house.

'She's right, you know,' Lark said coolly.

Iakas sighed. 'I know, but it gets on my nerves the way she quotes him every other second as though she can't think for herself.'

'You're just mad because no one quotes you like that.'

Iakas gave him a wry smile. 'You're wrong, though. I don't aspire to leadership exactly because having a leader means everyone else turns into a mush-brained follower. If I were a leader, I would want followers with brains and voices of their own. I would want them to argue so that I could argue back and hone my argument, and if on the rare occasion someone was more right than me, I would concede it and praise them.'

'Sounds good in theory,' Lark said. 'Only seeing as how you're so opposed to the roofies becoming a proper order, I guess you are not likely to set out to be their enlightened leader.'

Iakas sat back against the smooth warm chimney pot and watched rain slant past their protected niche. It was not so much that she opposed the roofies forming an order, but how it was happening. She had taken to the roofs precisely to get away from people telling her what to do. The rooftops meant freedom to Iakas and many of the others, Arrow included. They had come to symbolise a life that was lived above the level of ordinary lives. Roofies saw themselves as philosophers and dreamers and they were proud of their unworldliness. Roofies didn't think about food until they were hungry. They didn't think about warm clothes until it was winter and the snow started falling, then they would try to negotiate for clothes. They did this, as much as possible, from the rooftops. Those who chose the roofs rarely went down to the ground and when they had to, they tried to have as little to do with the ground dwellers as possible.

But Arrow had taken it all a step further. He wanted them to become mystics; a closed order of pure contemplation. He wanted them to demand that

Quentarans tithe to them. An idiotic notion if Iakas had ever heard one, because why would ordinary Quentarans agree to be taxed to support mystics who would tell them nothing and who despised them? But if she had told that to Arrow, he would say dreamily that he didn't expect ordinary people to understand. By ordinary, his tone suggested, he meant her.

To Iakas, Arrow was impractical to the point of downright stupidity at times, but the fact that he was extremely good-looking in the fragile, slender way that roofies admired, and had a lovely poetic line in rhetoric, kept all of the female roofies under his sway. And where the females went, their men followed.

Even Iakas had been attracted to Arrow at first, because he had seemed so much the opposite of her tough, mean father and thick-headed brothers. But dealing with her father and brothers had meant manipulating them using the cleverness in her nature, and this had given her a streak of pure prac-ticality that forced her to hear the emptiness behind

Arrow's fine sounding phrases. She kept thinking how downright dumb some of his ideas were. Like the idea of no roofie ever speaking to a ground dweller, or trading with one. How on earth were they to live, when the roofs did not provide all their needs? But tell that to Arrow and the others and she would be told that her mind was base and her concerns distressingly low.

The trouble was that Arrow never took into account that roofies were basically squatters. They were tolerated by the authorities and by the people upon whose roofs they built their roosts, because they were regarded as harmless and made no trouble. But there were people who didn't like them, and more than one roost had been thrown down and smashed to pieces when the roofie was away. If there was any sense in Arrow's idea of their becoming a proper order, it was only that they might be able to legitimise their precarious position and get the legal right to occupy the roofs of Quentaris. Which would mean they would have the right to defend themselves.

'Maybe I should stand against him,' she muttered.

'Are you serious?' Lark said, leaning forward to peer into her face.

'Someone should stand up for common sense, even on the roofs,' Iakas said. 'But I need a way to get their attention away from Arrow. Something really dramatic and exciting.'

'Excuse me ...' It was a timid voice and Iakas and Lark looked around until they saw a girl peeping over the lip of the roof, her hair plastered wetly to her scalp. She must be standing on one of the windowsills; in this rain, the sill would be slippery.

'Get down,' Iakas said sharply, keeping her voice low because she didn't want to be heard speaking to a ground dweller.

'Please,' the girl gasped. 'There is someone coming that needs your help.'

That made Iakas sit up because very occasionally, a roofie fell. 'Is it a roofie?'

The girl shook her head. 'Not a roofie. An angel! He ... he came through a rift.'

Iakas shook her head firmly, wondering what an

angel was. 'Roofies don't have anything to do with the rift caves.'

'But … he has wings!' the girl said desperately, and Iakas could see that her fingertips were white from the strain of hanging on.

Iakas's heart bounded in her chest as the sense of the girl's words penetrated. 'A man *with wings*?'

The girl nodded and then paled and Iakas guessed her fingers were slipping. 'Go down,' she ordered. 'I will come.'

'You're not going down?' Lark demanded in disbelief when the girl had withdrawn her head. 'How do you ever expect the roofies to follow you if you are seen with your feet on the ground?'

'Lark, did you hear what she said? A human with wings. Isn't that just the sort of thing that would get the attention of all roofies? Isn't it what we all secretly long for, despite Arrow's talk about minds with wings?'

Lark thought of his old dream of flying up to the clouds and realised he hadn't had it in a long time. Waking from his reverie, he found that Iakas had gone. She was not the most graceful or beautiful of roofies, but no one moved more lightly than she did.

⇒

Iakas seemed to those below to glide down, so swiftly and surely did she descend. Then she was on the ground, and despite everything, she felt a strange thrilled shock, for she had not set foot on the ground for more than two years.

Ignoring the slight, soaked girl who had summoned her from the roofs, Iakas leaned between the rift guards to look at the enormous unconscious man they carried. He was wrapped in a sodden grey cloak and although the rain had washed some of the blood from his face, he was a mess. He had wings all right, heavy with rain, and one of them hung down battered and broken. His breathing was very laboured.

'Is he dying?' Iakas demanded, her voice harsh to hide her astonishment at his beauty. *At his shining white wings!*

'We don't know, but if you will take him and undertake to care for him, I will go and get a healer.'

Glancing at the speaker, Iakas took in the colours of his armband and boots and realised that, unlike the rift guards who carried the winged man, he was one of the subterranean adventurers that dwelt under the surface of Quentaris. He went on, 'I am Igorik and this is my brother Red.' He gestured at one of the rift guards who was obviously his twin. Then he turned to point at the shivering girl. 'This is Eely, who found him. She …'

'I don't care what your names are, drainer. I will undertake to care for the winged man if you can lift him up to the roof.' Her voice was colder than she intended because she knew that even worse than touching the ground, was inviting ground dwellers onto the roofs. And a drainer! But there was no way that she could get the winged man up there herself, and this was her chance to put an end to Arrow's increasing dominance of the rooftops.

⋽

It took more than an hour to get the winged man to her roost, despite the soothsayers allowing the rift guards and the drainer to bring him through the building. The guards had hurried off at once with an air of urgency and then the big drainer, Igorik, went to get a healer. The girl that had come up onto the roof to get her had looked like she might linger, but Lark had hissed at her to go back to the ground where she belonged, and she had gone too, creeping away like a mouse.

When they were alone, Lark asked how they were supposed to pay the healer since roofies made it a point of honour to have nothing to do with money.

'I have coin from when I came up onto the roofs,' Iakas said, and ignored the gasp this occasioned, her mind occupied with trying to clean and dry the giant man as best she could. She shot a glare at the hovering Lark. 'Stop gaping and go and get your blankets.'

'But ...'

'But what?' Iakas scowled at him and he nodded and vanished.

Left alone with the winged man, Iakas ceased her cleaning and covered him with her dry cloak, knowing that the bits of him that most needed cleaning were his wounds and she knew too little to touch them. Bad enough that he had been hauled about so much, but there was nothing else they could have done. The soothsayers would have agreed that he could stay in the top room of their guild house, for they, too, had been struck by the winged man's extraordinary beauty, but Iakas was now convinced that the winged man belonged with the roofies. When she had said as much, the soothsayers had nodded at one another in that mysterious knowing way they had that always infuriated her because it implied that they had foreseen her response.

Iakas stared into the winged man's face thinking that he was beautiful, but not in the pale almost feminine way that Arrow was beautiful. His beauty was entirely masculine, as was his body which was strongly muscled but not in that exaggerated, bloated way that some men were muscled.

Her eyes were drawn to his mouth, and she found herself wondering what it would be like to kiss it and to be kissed back. She tried to imagine it, but something in her shivered at the thought of touching that wide curving mouth. Without making a conscious decision, Iakas bent over the winged man, but

when she was less than a finger's breadth away, she
hesitated.

And that was when he woke.

His eyes were a startling blue, and compelling.
'Where is she?' he rasped. 'The beauteous Lady who
saved me from the monster.'

'Uh,' Iakas blinked, falling back. 'I don't know of
any beauteous lady.' *Or any monster*, she thought.
He was clearly delirious. 'Just rest and you'll feel
better in a while.'

'My wings ...' the winged man said, and tried to
move, then he groaned and fell still.

'You're badly hurt,' Iakas said. 'You must lie still
until the healer comes.'

'Where am I?' the winged man asked.

Iakas decided that talk would hurt him less than
movement so she said, 'You are in the city of
Quentaris. You came through the rift from your
world. Did a monster attack you there?'

'I was thrown into the Aurora vortex and when I
woke there was a foul creature leaning over me. The
foulness of her face ...' His heartfelt horror was
enough to make Iakas glad she had not seen it.

She shook her head. 'You're safe now. I am Iakas and you are in my roost. When the healer comes he will clean your wounds and give you something for the pain.'

'The Lady!' The winged man tried to sit up again, and again he fell back with a moan. He looked at Iakas. 'Please, you must bring her to me. I ... I would thank her for her courage.'

'I don't think ...' Iakas began, then she frowned, remembering the sodden blonde girl with her bland wide face and dullard's eyes. The drainer claimed she had found the winged man, but she was neither beautiful nor a Lady. 'I will see if she can be found,' she said at last. This seemed to comfort the winged man, for he relaxed. She noticed then that his harsh breathing seemed to have eased slightly.

'What is going on here, Iakas?'

Iakas froze, because it was Arrow's mellifluous voice. She turned to find the pale roofie staring at her from the opening to the roost. Behind him, hovering shamefaced and uneasy, was Lark. Iakas controlled her anger. 'I am sure Lark has told you what is going on,' Iakas said with the faint sarcasm she had taken to using to deflect Arrow's presumptions. 'The question is why are you here?'

Arrow bridled. 'I am merely concerned when earthies are invited onto our roofs.'

'*Our* roofs,' Iakas said. 'It is strange how we who once called the roofs free, now claim them like any ground dweller claims his piece of dirt.' She disliked the term *earthie* because Arrow used it so often.

Arrow's eyes narrowed. 'If you do not like the way the roofs work, you can always go down to earth,' he said.

Iakas held onto her temper with difficulty, because to lose it would be to concede victory to Arrow. Her voice, when she spoke, was calm. 'I was not aware I needed your advice in this or any other matter, roofie,' she said, emphasising the last word because Arrow's followers had taken to calling him Master.

There was anger in Arrow's eyes now, and his voice was icy. 'The roofs belong to us. To roofies. The question is whether or not you are a true roofie or merely an earthie with delusions of grandeur.'

Iakas might have flown at him then and doomed

herself because roofies were avowed pacifists, but the winged man groaned and twisted on his pallet. Arrow came closer and his eyes widened as he took in the size of the winged man and his astonishing beauty.

'His wings are shining,' he murmured.

'One of them is badly hurt,' Iakas said. 'A healer is coming …'

Arrow drew himself up. 'You would bring yet another earthie here?'

'A healer,' Iakas stressed, her temper rising again, but then she saw, as Arrow did not, that some of his followers had arrived and were easing through the roost flap behind him to gaze in wonder at the winged man. 'Unless you would advise that we let one of our own die.'

'Our own?' Arrow echoed.

'Do we not regard ourselves as kindred to the wind and the winged?' Iakas asked, so softly that Arrow was alerted. He turned and when he saw the other roofies, his expression melted into a sweetness that made Iakas's teeth ache.

'Of course we do, Iakas. But it remains to be seen if your winged man lives or dies.'

'*My* winged man will live, I promise you that,' Iakas said, seizing on the word triumphantly, and Arrow's pale cheeks flushed with the realisation that in naming the winged man to Iakas, he had disqualified himself from claiming him.

He withdrew, herding his followers before him. 'Then we will leave you to your winged man, Iakas,' he said. 'We have deep matters to discuss and we do not wish to encounter the earthie that you have invited to heal our winged brother.'

There were a few scandalised looks at this, but even through the light rain still falling, Iakas saw that more than a few of the roofies looked back, their eyes alight with curiosity and wonder. And she knew she had been right. If the winged man lived and flew, she would be able to topple Arrow from his pinnacle.

If he lived, and right now, there was no certainty of that, despite her confident avowal to Arrow.

'Lady, where are you?' the winged man moaned.

The Wingstone

'Where is it?' Nonaerom demanded. To speak with such force made every fibre in his flesh scream, but he stifled his pain and glared at the compact dark-haired woman yawning and blinking at him, her eyes dull with exhaustion.

In her turn, Iakas fought her weariness to note that the winged man looked a good deal better than on the night before.

The healer had come and gone on dusk, taking her coin and promising to return on another day to examine the wounds once the swelling had gone down. He had assured Iakas that there were no internal injuries and no broken bones to worry about. The beating had been savage but the real focus of it had been the damaged wing. He had refused to look at it more than superficially though, saying that wings must be treated by one familiar with their structure. A bird healer, and there was only one of those in Quentaris at present; he was Brodan, falconer to the Nibhellines. Seeing Iakas's dismay, the healer had said soothingly that he thought the famously haughty falconer would be likely to come out of curiosity if nothing else. He would speak with the man himself. In the meantime, he had given Iakas a syrupy liquid to soak into the wing, saying this would numb it until Brodan arrived.

The winged man had slept restlessly throughout the first part of a night full of rain that followed, moaning in pain until the fever predicted by the healer broke. When he lay still at last and deeply asleep, Iakas had gently soaked his battered wing in the sweet scented syrup. Then she had bathed him, enjoying the illicit pleasure of touching such a splendid body while its owner lay sleeping.

She had finally fallen asleep herself near dawn, only to be wakened by the winged man's cry. 'Where is what?' she asked now.

'The wingstone. I would never have let it go, no matter what was done to me.'

Still half asleep, Iakas began to cast about in the bedding, but the winged man caught her hand in his enormous grasp, and even as she marvelled at the softness of his skin, she felt a moment of fear, knowing that he could crush her bones if he wished.

'I told you, I would not have let it fall from my hand, woman. It must have been taken from me.'

Iakas drew herself up indignantly. 'I did not take anything from you. Nor would any roofie steal from you. We have no interest in material things.' Inwardly she mocked herself for sounding as pompous as Arrow.

The winged man nodded. 'I am sorry. I see that you have cared for me and I thank you. I had something with me when I ... when I came here. A precious thing it was, a stone which has the shape of a small feather. It is called the wingstone by my people and it is vital to us. It must be found.'

'It might have fallen from your hand as you were carried here,' Iakas said. 'I will ask the guards who brought you. Maybe it is still in the rift cave where they found you. Or they might have taken it from you, fearing that you would let it fall as they bore you along.'

'Ask them now. It is vital that it be found.'

'I can't leave you alone,' Iakas said firmly. 'When Lark returns with food, I will send him. In the meantime, I have nothing to offer you but water.'

'I am thirsty,' the winged man said, and Iakas lifted his head in her arms, feeling the golden softness of his hair against her cheek as she tilted a mug so that he could drink. 'Thank you,' he said courteously as she lay his head back against the pillow.

'What is your name?' Iakas asked.

'I am Nonaerom, Prince of the Cloudlands. I was attacked and sent to this place.'

'Who attacked you?' Iakas asked, agog at the thought that she had a winged man who was also a prince. Wait until Arrow heard that!

'Land walkers,' Nonaerom said. 'I was visiting Landfall City on the king's behalf when I was waylaid. Many land walkers resent the Cloudlands and those of us who dwell there. They claim that we are parasites who set ourselves above them and use them as slaves. It is not true, of course. We serve them by creating beauty to feed them and to feed the wingstone. Alas I had not time enough to tell them that I bore the wingstone, for even the land walkers revere it for its great power. They will know its lack now, though, for their city as well as the Cloudlands was warmed and lit by its grace.'

'How big is the wingstone?' Iakas asked.

'Small,' he said. 'Very small and very perfect. I was its appointed bearer and I had held it for many months without its slipping away from me.'

'Slipping away? You talk like it's alive.'

'I do not know if it lives in the sense that you or I live, or even as a tree lives, but it lives.'

'How do you know?' Iakas asked.

'It needs to be fed, though in these times it had been increasingly difficult to hold and to feed.'

'What does it eat?' Iakas asked, now trying to imagine a rock with teeth.

'It feeds on beauty, but perhaps feed is not the right word either. It is better to say that as far as we can tell, the wingstone needs beauty. It thrives when it is exposed to it, and its ability to produce the power we need for our cities rises or falls depending on how well it thrives.' He frowned and then went on, seeming to Iakas to speak more to himself than to her now. 'It may be because land walkers' cities have received less of its power than was traditional, resentment has produced aberrant personalities such as those that attacked me. They blame the winged folk for failing to content the wingstone. Of course we did not inform them of how difficult and elusive the wingstone has become of late.'

'Why not?' Iakas wondered.

Nonaerom gave her a cool look. 'It was not their

affair. Care of the wingstone belongs to winged folk. Why else would its truest shape be that of a feather?'

Iakas was puzzled and would have asked what he meant by its truest shape, but at that moment Lark arrived with a small bag of food. 'Peaches and chestnuts,' he announced, then his eyes widened as he noticed that the winged man was awake.

'Greetings, O Winged One,' he said reverently, and bowed gracefully enough to please Nonaerom's sharp aesthetics. Iakas saw the slight nod Nonaerom gave him and felt a sharp stab of jealousy, for not once had he nodded so at her.

'This is Lark,' she said. 'And I am Iakas. We are roofies and we will serve you until you are well, and can ...'

'I don't mean to interrupt you mid-worship,' said a voice.

Iakas swung around in time to see the craggy-faced red-haired rift guard whose twin had been the sour-looking drainer. She hid her anger at his invasion and said civilly, 'Thank you, guard, for sending the healer.'

'It was Igorik who fetched him, but you would

have to go down to Lower Quentaris to thank him, so I will convey your words to him when I see him next.' The red-haired man's words were perfectly polite, but there was a thread of amusement in them that made Iakas feel hot and furious.

'Do so,' she said coolly, hoping her anger did not show. She had the annoying feeling that knowing he had roused her would only amuse the red-haired guard. 'And now, what do you want?'

'Want?' His eyes flashed laughter at her. 'I want nothing. I merely came to see if there was anything you wanted from me.'

His voice was so openly and outrageously suggestive that Iakas actually bit her tongue to keep herself from saying the words forming in her mind. 'I want nothing,' she managed to say shortly. 'And as you see, the winged man is in good hands, so you may leave without thinking of him further.'

'Oh, I could do that easily enough, but my superiors have a pernickety habit of wanting to keep tabs on rift travellers.' Without giving Iakas time to say anything else, he turned and bowed slightly to Nonaerom, and this time there was no mockery in him. 'I am Redarick, Sir, and my superiors wish to know which world you hail from, and if there is regular trafficking with other worlds there.'

'I am Prince Nonaerom, and the people of my world have no dealings with other worlds,' Nonaerom said. 'Indeed I thought that I was to die when I was flung into the Aurora vortex. That is what my attackers desired.' Then his serenity crumbled and they both saw the agony in his eyes. 'I am dead if I am never to see the Cloudlands again.'

'Of course you can see the Cloudlands, Prince, if they are where you came from,' Red said easily. 'Once you are well, we will speak with a guide and figure out exactly how you can get back to your world. But my superiors will want to speak with you about your world before that can happen. If there is to be any future trade or communication through the rift, we must know what to expect.'

Nonaerom had heard only the words that mattered and his eyes blazed. 'I can return?'

'Of course you can,' Iakas said quickly, trying to turn his attention back to her.

But Nonaerom's shoulders slumped. 'No. It is no

good. I cannot return without the wingstone. I was its bearer and I will be rightly reviled for losing it.'

'The wingstone?' Red asked, and Iakas explained, for Nonaerom had sunk his head in his hands. Red shrugged. 'I don't see why we couldn't find it. It sounds pretty distinctive and you must have dropped it on the way from the cave to here. We can just retrace your steps back to the rift cave. Like as not it will still be there.'

Nonaerom lifted his head from his hands. 'I do not believe I dropped the stone. I had trained myself too hard and long never to loosen my grip. Even in my sleep, I would have held it. It must have been taken from me.'

Red was frowning in thought now. 'I will ask Eely. She might have taken it.'

'She stole it …' Nonaerom began, but Red gave him a fierce look and he fell silent at once.

'Eely found you and she fought off a harpy to keep you safe. If she took it, she meant only to take care of it for you. She probably would have given it back except your roofie friends pushed her out of here so fast yesterday.' He cast a swift look at Iakas, who flushed to remember that Lark *had* all but pushed the girl out. After she had fought off a harpy!

'The Beauteous Lady!' Nonaerom breathed. 'That is her name? Eely? Yes, the stone would have wanted to go to her because of her great beauty. It might even have slipped from me to her without her knowing it.'

Red exchanged a look with Iakas, then he said, 'Uh, Eely is not a Lady, Nonaerom. She is …'

'I wish to see her,' Nonaerom announced, suddenly grandiose. 'Bring her to me at once.' He was looking at Iakas, who resented being given orders, but she could hardly protest since she had only just told the winged man that she was at his service.

She turned to Red. 'Tell her to come here for the sake of the Winged Prince whose life she saved.'

Red's eyes glinted dangerously and she thought he would refuse, but he nodded and departed with no more than a sardonic bow. Iakas heaved a sigh of relief when he was gone, and hoped he would send the girl alone. But no matter. Nonaerom would quickly see that he had made a mistake in thinking the dullard a beauteous Lady. He would claim his wingstone, and then she would convince him to remain with the roofies until he was healed.

And while he waited, she would ask him to speak to the roofies of the Cloudlands and of flying, so that he would fire their imaginations and they would stop listening to Arrow's morbid talk of solitude and prayer and closed orders. She would be at his side whenever he addressed the others, to introduce him, and soon the others would see her as his special chosen helper. She could just imagine how Nonaerom would look with them all gathered about his feet as he declaimed, the sun increasing the strange brightness of his wings, and the nimbus of his hair floating about him. And when he was gone, it was the sight of her they would long for, because she would be associated forever with the winged man.

In a way it would be perfect that he would stay only long enough to burn his image into their minds, then he would forever be associated with the deepest yearning that Iakas thought was the truest expression of a roofie's soul. Wasn't it that very yearning that caused them to climb to the roofs?

⇒

It was not until the following morning that Red had the opportunity to speak with Eely, and when he arrived, he found Cora furiously upbraiding her.

'Where were you all night?' she demanded.

'I walked,' Eely said in a dreamy voice that made Red feel that part of her was still wandering. 'I stopped to help at the soup kitchen. You know, the place where …'

Cora interrupted impatiently. 'Eely, I want to know what possessed you to stay out all night? Don't you know I was worried out of my mind?'

Eely hung her head. 'I … don't know. I was thinking about everything. About the angel and about your being made a captain. I am a burden, I know.'

'Oh for goodness sake!' Cora flung up her hands in frustration. 'There are no angels. They're just part of some rift-travellers' story that Mama told you!'

The brightness died from Eely's face, and suddenly she looked very small and very tired. Red felt a flash of anger at Cora, whom he usually admired. He went down on one knee beside Eely and put his hand on her shoulder, and she turned a blank face to him.

'I don't know if he is an angel, Eely, but he wants to see you. He wants to thank you for saving his life.'

She shook her head. 'You must have made a mistake. He wouldn't want me.'

'He does. He asked for you.' Red hesitated, then he said, 'And Eely, he wants to ask if you took something out of his hand or found it on the ground in the cave. It was a little stone shaped like a feather. Clear like glass ...'

'It was a crystal feather,' Eely said softly. 'The angel banged his hand on the wall and it just flew into my lap.' She gave a soft giggle. 'No, of course it didn't fly, but it seemed like that. And I held it up and oh it sparkled so. I put it in my pocket.' She frowned. 'I thought I did, but later when I went to get it out and give it back to the angel, it wasn't there.'

Red stifled a sigh. 'Never mind, it must have fallen out of your pocket when you climbed up to talk to the roofies. Well, I will find it, but come now and you can tell him what happened.'

Eely shook her head. 'He will be angry that I lost it.'

'No he won't,' Red said firmly.

'What is this stone?' Cora asked in her official voice. 'Is it some kind of weapon?'

'I don't think so. It's mostly a symbol, like a crown. Oh, it's also a source of power, apparently. Nonaerom told the roofie we left him with that it provided light and heat to at least two cities.'

'That sort of power must have weapon applications,' Cora said. 'It had better be found at once. Eely can find her own way to the roof of the Soothsayers' Guild. You can …'

But Red shook his head. 'Cora, I'm off duty and I've had a night stretch. The regulations say: *a guard shall not be permitted to perform his duties for so long a period that he cannot serve them fully and well.'*

Cora gave him a look. 'Since when have you been a stickler for rules?'

'Since now,' Red said, taking Eely's arm.

'Wait just a minute, Red. Eely is my little sister and I think it is about time I took a look at this winged man.'

The
Search
for Beauty

Nonaerom stared at the slight girl standing timidly before him, taking in the stained bodice of her dress, the lank hair, the awkward stance and the strangely bland face with its pale, limpid eyes. He could see that she was simple, even if her stumbling words had not revealed it. So the transcendent beauty had been an illusion after all, somehow superimposed over this girl. But for all his disappointment, Nonaerom was not cruel and whatever she was, this poor child had saved his life. So he lifted his hand.

Shyly, Eely put her small, rather grubby hand in his, thinking that if she died in that moment, her life would have served its purpose. It was not the sort of thought she would normally have, and she attributed it to the angel's grace.

'My Lady, your courage was very bright,' Nonaerom said gravely.

'What about the wingstone?' Iakas asked.

Eely's face fell at once. 'I am so sorry, Angel. You hit your hand on the wall and it fell into my lap. I put it into my pocket to give you later, but it must have fallen out …' She stopped because the angel was shaking his head.

'Do not blame yourself, child. It would take more than a pocket to hold the wingstone. I myself held it by right, and yet I must needs hold it at all times, conscious or unconscious, never loosening my grip for a single second.'

'Are you saying that it got out of her pocket on its own?' Cora asked sceptically.

'It's alive,' Iakas told her. 'Or anyway, Prince Nonaerom says it has a will of its own.'

'You mean it is some sort of animal?' Cora persisted.

She was looking at Nonaerom, who said, 'It is not a creature, yet it shifts from place to place and hand to hand, though no one ever sees it move. It snatches at opportunities which bring it closer to where it wants to be. Eely might have bent to get up and it would have rolled easily out of her pocket.'

'Then it will be in the cave where she found you,' Red said, half rising.

'Not necessarily,' Nonaerom said. 'It could just as easily have rolled from the child's pocket into yours, or into someone else's.'

'How could it roll when it is shaped like a feather?'

'Because it is not always that shape,' Nonaerom said somewhat wearily.

'You said it shifts and changes to get closer to

what it wants,' Red said slowly. 'What would it want to be close to, exactly?'

Nonaerom looked momentarily so sorrowful that even Cora felt a twinge of pity for him. 'It desires beauty,' he said softly.

'Beauty?' Cora echoed in much the same tone as she might have said *dung*.

'I cannot say it more clearly than that,' Nonaerom told her. 'We learned of its need over the eons since it came to the hands of the winged folk and we have shaped our whole culture to provide for that need. And the land walkers saw that we were able to look after the wingstone and did not dispute that we held it. For hundreds of years, the wingstone was content, but in the last hundred years, it has seemed restless and no effort made, even by our finest artists, can seem to satisfy it.'

'Is it possible that the wingstone wants something here in Quentaris?' Iakas said.

Nonaerom gave her a cold look. 'Do you think there can be more beauty in this city than in the

Cloudlands where every person and every thing is dedicated to beauty?'

Iakas flushed. 'I didn't mean that. I just wondered if there was something here that might have attracted it.'

The haughty pride faded from his handsome face into a sort of hopeless despair. 'If there is beauty here, that is where you will find the wingstone.'

'Then the roofies will find it for you, for no one sees further and more clearly than we do,' Iakas declared fiercely. She directed this to the roofies that had been gathering outside the open flap of the roost, and they erupted into excited agreement.

Iakas judged it yet another sign that Arrow's imposed serenity was beginning to wear thin on all but the most devout. The idea of a hunt thrilled them, and since their hunt centred on the search for a desperately important object belonging to a winged prince, she doubted that Arrow would risk openly disapproving. But just in case, the sooner the hunt began the better.

'Tell us what to look for,' she said to Nonaerom.

He looked at her, and seeing the yearning in his eyes, a fist seemed to clench around her heart and squeeze.

'The wingstone reshapes itself to suit its surroundings, unless it is touched by one who knows its truest shape,' he said. 'That means that if it rests in a garden, then it will seem to be a flower, or a butterfly or maybe a particularly pretty stone. If it rests among jewels, then it will be the brightest among them, or perhaps it will be the cushion they rest upon.'

'I could speak to the Venerable Lightfingers,' Red said. 'The head of the Thieves' Guild will certainly know where the best jewels are, even if they are hidden.'

'I'll speak to the head of the Fences' Guild as well,' Cora said. 'Let them know what we are looking for because if a jewel appears, it's very likely to be thought to be stolen and it may be traded.'

'What about the City Watch?' asked one of the roofies excitedly. 'It might just have been handed in.'

'I'll ask Commander Storm, but I wouldn't bet on people handing in a jewel of great beauty,' Red said.

'Come to think of it, it may be that no one picked it up. Remember it was raining buckets yesterday and the streets were all but deserted. I'll go and speak to Igorik.'

'You think a stone that loves beauty would end up under the earth?' Iakas sneered.

Red gave her a look devoid of his usual humour. 'Since most stones of beauty are born of the earth, I don't think they would despise it, roofie.' Red turned back to Nonaerom, leaving Iakas stinging at the rebuke in his tone. 'But I meant that the stone might have washed into the drains. Almost everything that is lost ends up in Lower Quentaris. And the drainers are always finding jewels and coins, so it would be in beautiful and costly company. I'll ask the Divers' Guild too, because it might have fallen down into the submerged caves.'

Nonaerom nodded, but vaguely, as if his thoughts were elsewhere.

Iakas fought with jealousy and resentment at the interference of the red-haired guard, but she managed to quell it because he had a point. And there was something else. She had intended this search to be exclusively a roofie hunt, but she couldn't help but be amazed at how easily the roofies were now discussing possible locations of the wingstone with the two rift guards. There was no hint of their usual aloofness and the knowledge that this would have appalled Arrow restored her good humour. Nevertheless she was not going to let this moment be snatched from her.

She stood up, the movement drawing all their eyes as she had intended. 'All right, let's not waste time talking,' she said. 'Let's search.'

Making her way agilely across the roofs towards the Square of Dreams, Iakas dismissed the irritating Red and pondered her reactions to Nonaerom. At first, she had not thought of the winged man as anything more than a symbol which she could use to rally the roofies and draw them from Arrow's numbing influence. But watching him sleep and washing his body, she had come to feel ... Well, that was the trouble. She didn't really know what she felt. She was attracted to him and why not, for he was beautiful.

But she was not ordinarily drawn to handsome men. In her experience, they were like Arrow, so languidly aware of his beauty and certain of the advantage it gave him over less ravishing individuals, that he was like dealing with a jellyfish. Arrow could talk but his were almost always beautiful words saying nothing. Then there were good-looking men who were stupid simply because they had never bothered to develop their minds or skills. The truth was that Iakas was attracted to strength of character rather than to physical beauty, because so often beauty in people hid a great vacancy, unlike beauty in things or buildings. She had always been drawn to sharp, tricky minds with edges that could sometimes stab or even cut you. Or men who confounded or confused her because she couldn't quite figure them out.

Nonaerom was a mystery, but he was more elusive than complex. Of course, it might be that in his own world among his own people, he would be different, but she was not so sure about that either, because of what he had just now said about his people being devoted to beauty. It occurred to her that she had not once seen Nonaerom laugh, and that might be at the heart of her ambivalence about him. For her, laughter was essential, maybe because she was so serious. She needed someone to be able to make her laugh.

She sighed and noticed that she was shaking her head. She made herself stop because it was a sure sign of madness to be muttering and shaking her head to herself. The trouble was that these days, it seemed like the only person she had to talk to was herself. She had friends among the other roofies, but none of them really discussed or argued about things in a way that tested her. They all seemed so passive to her and so dully serene. It might be partly because Arrow was always telling the roofies they must strive for harmony and peace above all things. It sounded lovely, but the reality of it was that when she asked what they thought about something, the other roofies would simply offer a watered down version of what she had said, as if they had no minds of their own. But maybe it wasn't just Arrow. Maybe it was also the way roofies lived apart from other people. It might even be that Arrow himself was a product of that strange emptiness at the heart of roofie lives rather than the one who was making it happen.

The only thing any of them did was to compose poetry to the skies and the stars and clouds and the wind. It was hearing one of the roofies recite his poem to the wind that had filled her with such a rush of joyous certainty that this life was for her. She did not regret that choice, but these days it seemed to her that roofie poetry had become an empty mouthing of acceptable Arrow phrases and philosophies, rather than an expression of something important.

Iakas thought of the vivid interest in the faces of the roofies as they had discussed who would seek where for the wingstone. She had thought of their need to trade and of the advantages to be had from establishing themselves as an order, when she had argued against the policy of strict separation preached by Arrow. But maybe there was more than that to be gained by having a dialogue with ground dwellers.

She came to a wide gap between roofs and some

strange energy coursing through her made her eschew the poles and decorative wires running from rooftop to rooftop, which most roofies used to scale wide gaps. She could make the jump, she told herself, measuring it with her sure roofie's eye. The gap was wide but it was a matter of pride to her that few could leap as well as she, though Arrow always sneered at her skill, calling it *merely athletic*.

Readying herself for the jump, she pushed Arrow, her confusion about Nonaerom and her thoughts about the possibility of a roofie order from her mind. She crouched, folding her legs beneath her and feeling her muscles twitch with anticipation. Then she straightened her legs and leapt out, arching and lengthening her body so as to lessen wind resistance.

She crossed the gap in a long soaring moment that seemed to be elongated by the joy she felt. The moment her feet touched the roof, she sank into a ball to absorb the shock then at once, she spread her arms wide, flattening herself to the tiles. She stayed that way for a long still moment, then she rose, filled with exaltation and lightness at the knowledge that the wondrous jump had been nearly impossible, and yet she had made it.

She smiled, thinking there were some beauties that could only be felt by the one who created them.

≈

Coming to the Idler's Gardens, Iakas drew a deep breath before dropping lightly to the ground. This was the second time within a few days that she had set foot on the ground, and despite the fact that many of the other roofies would be doing the same thing for the first time in ages, she felt again the strange thrill of transgression as she began to move among the exquisite flower beds and statuary that had been her solace when she had dwelt on the ground with her earthbound family. If the wingstone was looking for beauty, this was where it would find it.

Iakas began to search, holding the image of the wingstone in her mind as Nonaerom had suggested, so that it would change when her fingers touched it.

7

To Fly

Red strode along, wondering what it was about the Thieves' Guild leader that always got on his nerves, despite their unlikely friendship. It was not that the Venerable Lightfingers was actually opposed to just about everything Red believed in, but the way he refused to say things outright. He was always hinting and expecting you to figure out what he meant. Why he could not simply say what he thought was beyond a mere rift guard who preferred truth to any form of clever evasion.

Red shrugged, telling himself as he always did, that thieves were evasive by nature and that was that.

And anyway he was too honest not to acknowledge that it was not really the meeting with the Venerable Lightfingers spoiling his mood. It was Iakas.

He thought about the roofie with her dark spiky hair that so perfectly reflected her prickly mind, and wondered exactly what it was about her that so attracted him. It was not like she was strictly beautiful, though there was something striking about her that eluded naming. But maybe more than how she looked, it was how she was. Right from the start he had noticed that there was an intensity in her that made her seem twice as alive as other roofies. The truth was, she didn't look like a roofie at all because most of them were slim and willowy and identically attractive in a blonde wispy way. Iakas seemed too real and definite, too fierce to be a roofie.

If anything, she reminded him of one of the journeyman earth magicians, compact and taciturn and frowningly intense as they always seemed to be. But at the same time, she didn't have their cloddish stubbornness, or their complete practicality. There was something in the way her mind worked that was light and free and swift as a bird darting about in the treetops. That quicksilver brightness was what he was most drawn to, because he had never met anyone who thought like that before.

Red sighed and grinned at himself, thinking that he was acting like a lovesick teenager. The fact was that he had been attracted to the infuriating Iakas from the start, but the strength of his attraction had not hit him until he had been walking along the street a few days before, and had happened to glance up and see her crouched perilously at the edge of a roof. He had almost cried out in alarm, but the look of grim determination on her face made him realise that she was on the verge of making an impossible jump to the next roof, and if he shouted, she might fall.

He felt sick all over again, remembering his horror and helplessness as she gathered herself to make the impossible jump. He had held his breath as she leapt, and then she stretched out into a shape of such grace that he had been unable to sleep since for thinking of it. That image of her superimposed against the sky seemed to insert itself into his mind at the most peculiar and inappropriate moments so that twice today, Cora had reprimanded him for his failure to listen.

Alternating with that image of her flying across the sky, was the moment in which she had landed, folding neatly into herself like a little cat, all claws and spiky fluff. She had just made it to the edge and fearing that she would fall back, he had stepped forward with some confused and idiotic notion of catching her. Except she didn't fall. She flattened herself to the roof for a moment, and then she rose and stepped lightly over the peak of the roof without even looking down.

He stood there for a long time after she had gone, gazing up at the gap between the two buildings and feeling his blood fizz. Who would have ever thought love would come like a sneaky gut punch? Because love was what it was. What it had to be. The next morning when they had met with the soothsayers to see if they could offer any omens that would help in the search for the wingstone, he had stared at Iakas, amazed that she could light such a fire in him without knowing it. She had finally glared at him and asked what he thought he was looking at. He laughed to remember the indignant look on her face when he said he was still trying to work that out. He wondered what exactly it was about him that repelled her, other than that he was not a stunningly handsome, nine-foot-high, winged prince. He had tried holding his tongue when something sarcastic came to his mind, but it was too hard to resist provoking her. He liked the way her eyes flashed with anger, and she was no mean wit when it came to answering him back, either. She was like a little firecracker spitting with fury and brightness and sparking fire, and he couldn't help wondering what it would be like to hold that fire close in his arms. He had the feeling that kissing her might be like sharing that arching leap into nothingness, and the thought of it made him feel dizzy.

He might even have been crazy enough to go after her when she disappeared after that incredible jump, but fortunately for him, Eely had happened along looking so unusually happy that he had been prompted to ask where she had been. She told him that she had been to the Paupers' market to get some fruit for Nonaerom.

'I like it there,' she had confided shyly. 'They smile at one another and sing and tell stories as they work. The people there are happy,' she added as if this were a rarity.

Which maybe it was. But even in being able to express these thoughts, Eely had changed.

It was funny how much confidence she had gained from her association with Nonaerom. She seemed to carry herself less awkwardly now that people were not always dismissing or ignoring her. Even Iakas had stopped being stand-offish because Eely was so diffident and eager to help. It was the roofie who had suggested that Eely stay with Nonaerom while the rest of them searched for the wingstone.

Iakas ...

Red sighed again and decided he had better think some different thoughts since he would be seeing her in about ten minutes. And of course she would have plenty of scorn to pour on his efforts since they had led to nothing. It didn't help that his main motive in wanting to find the wingstone was to beat Iakas to it. A downright stupid motive, since it was hardly likely to endear him to her. But there it was. She roused in him a desire to conquer as much as to kiss, and that was not at all his usual style. Generally he made his romantic approaches with lazy amusement and was not that troubled if he was spurned. But his feelings for Iakas went deeper than usual and seemed to have roused primitive instincts that he had not known he possessed.

He frowned, wondering if Igorik had had any luck in locating the wingstone. They were to meet for a pie in the market that evening, but Red was sure his brother would have sent word if he had any good news to report. Besides, he would have *felt* it.

He was passing the house of Rad de La'rel, and that reminded him that he had promised Nonaerom to see if one of the guides would come to speak with him. He might as well do it now, he decided. A visit from a guide might cheer the winged man, who had grown increasingly morose with their continued failure to find the wingstone, despite the fact that the Thieves' Guild, the Fences' Guild, the roofies and most of the City Watch and rift guard were searching for it, not to mention the drainers.

It was a pity the soothsayers had not been able to offer any clear help, but that was the way with fore-tellings. They were either so specific that you need not have been told what you could have used your common sense to figure out, or they were so obscure and mysterious that they might as well have been gibberish.

In this case, the soothsayer journeyman who had been given the task of seeking omens had gazed into his mirror then announced that the wingstone had found a deep shape, and had no desire to be found.

Of course there had been a lot more jabber and ges-
turing but that was the heart of it. Nonaerom had
shrugged his incomprehension when they told him.
The only thing Red had been able to think of was
that they ought to question the divers again.

In the end, Rad de La'rel agreed to come with him at
once.

It began to rain lightly again as they walked apace
through the streets, but in an unconvincing way that
made Red think it might stop soon. He was heartily
sick of rain. It was nice when the city was freshened
up and sluiced down by a brief shower, but this rain
had gone on for too long. It was getting so that it was
hard to believe in blue skies. Red's thoughts
returned to Iakas, who had told him contrarily that
she liked bad weather a whole lot better than dull
blue skies.

They had arrived at the roost, and Red let the
guide go ahead because he wanted to try controlling
his pounding heart before he had to face Iakas. Yet

the first person he set eyes on was Eely. She was sitting outside Iakas's roost and right then the rain stopped and a watery sun slipped from the clouds to bathe her in a soft pink light. She looked up and smiled at him, and he was genuinely startled at how lovely she looked.

'Hello Red,' she said, and he marvelled again at the change in her.

A few nights before, after Eely had gone off to her bed, he had stayed to have a drink with Cora and had made the mistake of wondering aloud if her sister was really a simpleton, or had just been neglected. Cora had snapped that Eely had never been neglected. *She* saw to that.

'I didn't mean that you neglect her welfare,' Red had answered. 'You care for her, of course, but you don't really care what she says or feels or thinks. You don't treat her as a person. No one does. Or they didn't until Nonaerom came along.'

He had stopped then, noticing the stricken look on Cora's usually placid face. He could have bitten his tongue off then, but who would have thought Cora would react like that? Unemotional, practical, competent Cora who was famous for having a level head when everyone else was falling about in hysterics. Commander Storm might have thought twice of her recommendation that Cora be promoted, had she seen the tears welling in the young woman's eyes.

There had been no point in taking it back because Red had spoken the truth. Until Nonaerom had come to Quentaris, Eely had barely existed in anyone's eyes. Now everyone greeted her when they came to speak with Nonaerom, who, at least in the beginning, had spoken often and with such longing and poetic enthusiasm of his precious Cloudlands, and of the cult of beauty among the winged folk, that roofies were not the only ones to come to hear him. There had been young men and women of all ranks and guilds, as more and more people learned of the presence of the otherworld prince with his shining wings and miraculous beauty. Even the Archon had sent a messenger to ask if he would come to dinner when he had recovered. But their failure to find the wingstone despite all efforts had stilled Nonaerom's poetry. And in his growing despair, he seemed to take comfort from Eely's quiet, devoted presence which demanded nothing of him, so that when she was away, he often asked where she was.

Not that she was away from him more than a few hours at a time. The only time Eely came down from the roofs lately was to get food from the Paupers' market, and to go home and bathe. So Cora had complained.

Recalling himself forcibly to the present, Red introduced Rad to Eely and noted with interest how the guide's eyes rested appreciatively on her face. Her smile faltered when he explained that he was a guide, though.

'You will guide him back to his own world?' she asked.

'I'm sure I can,' Rad said softly, misreading the anxiety in her eyes.

Eely nodded and said sadly, 'He will be glad. But you must wait to speak with him, for the Nibhelline falconer is looking at his hurt wing. Iakas is in there, too.' Eely said these last words to Red, and the compassion in her voice filled him with panic, because if even Eely saw how he felt about the roofie, then Iakas herself must know.

Gods! What if Iakas had spoken of it to Nonaerom? What if they had laughed together at him, never mind that he had decided that the winged man came from a culture that did not laugh. Red was trying to assemble the wit to withdraw when there was a great cry of anguish from within the roost. The flap opened and the Nibhelline falconer came out, his expression composed. Iakas followed, her face pale as milk.

'Are you sure that nothing can be done for the wing?' she asked. 'Maybe massage and oils …'

'They would do no more than soothe him,' Brodan said. 'Magic might heal the wing, but you know as well as I that healing magic has the tendency to change the object it is healing, because the spell itself will decide what needs fixing and it might not be the bit you intended. That is why it is so seldom used. Now, the payment?' He held out his hand.

Iakas thrust a gold royal at the falconer who pocketed it and nimbly climbed down from the roof.

'What happened?' Red asked Iakas gently, for she looked very small and shattered all at once. In that moment he realised that she was as young as Eely. It was not something he had noticed before because she always seemed so self-sufficient and decisive.

'The physic said that Nonaerom won't ever fly again. The wing is healing but it is too badly broken to be put back the way it was. He said … he said the best thing would be to remove both wings because the broken wing will make it hard for him to walk.'

Eely gasped and Red turned in time to see her faint dead away. It was Rad who caught her in his arms and carried her into the roost to lay her on the little pallet beside Nonaerom's bed. The guide's eyes widened when he straightened and saw the winged man with his head buried in his hands, ragged wing stretched awkwardly beside him.

Iakas was trembling by his side, and he put his arm around her. For a wonder, she did not reject him. She even leaned into him in a way that made him shudder and he took a deep breath, hoping it would be put down to a reaction at Nonaerom's plight. But all too soon she was turning away to Eely, who had woken and was moving to sit by Nonaerom. Iakas joined her as if they would sit vigil together.

'Perhaps I should go,' the guide murmured to Red. 'This is not the time for questions.'

'Stay,' Red said softly. 'Hearing you talk of him going home might comfort him.'

≋

'Home?' Nonaerom asked in a ravaged voice. 'There is no place for ugliness in the Cloudlands.'

'How could a broken wing make you ugly?' Eely asked softly.

Nonaerom gave her a look of passionate contempt. 'Can you not understand that my people cherish perfection? For us, a thing that is broken and cannot be mended is a thing which is ugly.'

Eely flinched as if he had slapped her, and Red felt a stab of anger at the winged man for his self-centred misery that did not allow compassion or sensitivity to others. 'Surely beauty is not so easily broken, unless by beauty you just mean a vase or a necklace or something,' he snapped, but Nonaerom did not seem to hear. 'Look ...' Red began, but the winged man turned a tragic face to him.

'Look! Yes, that is what they would do, then they would look away and never see me again. I cannot fly! Can you imagine what that means?'

Red thought of Iakas, flying, 'I can imagine how it would be to lose something precious. But, Nonaerom, you are a prince of your people and you said that you had a duty to return the wingstone. Isn't that still so?'

Nonaerom's drowning blue eyes were full of despair, but Red's words clearly touched him, for he drew himself up. 'If I had that duty to sustain me, it would be something, but you have not found the wingstone, have you, despite all of your efforts? It can only be that there is no beauty in this cursed world great enough to draw it, so it has perished.'

'You're wrong!' It was Iakas. She was standing and there was something in her eyes that had not been there before when she spoke to the winged prince. But there was no time for Red to decipher her expression because she was speaking again. 'There *is* beauty in our world, Prince, though maybe it is not the kind you and your people can love because it's not something you can see to worship. But I swore an oath and I meant it. I will not rest until the wingstone is found.' She glanced at Eely. 'Stay with him until I come back.'

She flung herself from the roost and Red went after her, leaving the rift guide to make his own farewell.

The Awakening

Nonaerom lay staring blankly up at the thin roof of Iakas's roost, his whole body heavy with despair. He wished that the land walkers had killed him outright rather than throwing him into the Aurora vortex.

He felt a soft hand on his arm and turned to find Eely bending over him with a mug.

He shook his head dully and watched her set the mug aside then smooth his blanket. She was not beautiful of course, not by any stretch of his imagination, but there was something about her that he had not noticed at first, perhaps because he had been so busy with his own urgent thoughts. Now everything in him felt still and quiet.

He watched her moving about the roost, finding a serenity in her gentle, graceful movements that soothed him. She looked up unexpectedly and broke into a radiant smile, as if merely being looked at by him filled her with joy.

She had thought he was an angel when she had first found him. Red had told him what that meant and he had been touched. Now, lying broken and ugly, he told himself that she was a simpleton who knew nothing, and yet he could not help but feel that *he* was the one missing something.

Red caught Iakas halfway down the street.

'Where are you going? We've looked everywhere already. You know that.'

'We haven't looked everywhere because we haven't found it!' she snarled, struggling in his grip.

'Then we've looked in the wrong places!' Red shouted.

She went limp in his hands and gaped at him. 'Wh ... what did you say?'

'I said ...' He stopped, struggling to recall.

'You said ... we had looked in the wrong places ...' Her voice was stronger now and the blind anger was gone from her eyes.

'Yes ...' Red said, trying to understand what had changed her mood so suddenly. Because now it was she who gripped *him*, pulling him close enough that he could see himself in her eyes; see his own bewilderment.

'I'm an idiot!' she hissed. 'The answer was staring me in the face and I didn't see it!'

'What?' he demanded.

Iakas laughed. 'You said back there that Nonaerom wasn't ugly the way he said, unless he

only meant beauty in the sense that a vase or a necklace was beautiful. But that's exactly what he did
mean. Maybe that's the only kind that they have
where he comes from. So we went to the Archon's
chef and to gardens and treasure houses and jew-
ellery hoards and to the songhouse to look for the
wingstone. All places where they have the kind of
beauty that Nonaerom meant. But maybe the wingstone was sick of that kind of beauty. Maybe that's
why it started getting restless and difficult back in
Nonaerom's world. I bet it's somewhere in Quentaris
that you can *feel* beauty rather than see it.'

'I see what you mean,' Red said, 'but it could be
anywhere then, including in all of the places we've
looked because sometimes you feel the beauty of
songs and gardens and statues as much as seeing or
hearing or smelling them. Or it could be in the
mountains because sometimes you feel the beauty of
them when you walk there.'

'I think we ought to start by looking where a lot
of people feel the sort of beauty you can *only* feel.
Because it could get those other kinds in the

Cloudlands.' She shrugged. 'What I'm trying to say is that maybe we ought to try to go somewhere that people go when they are happy or ...'

'Or inspired,' Red murmured, catching her excitement. 'The Studio maybe, where art is made, because making something beautiful makes you feel it. And what about the Orphans' Hospital? People who have been sick might find life beautiful.'

'Oh yes!' She hugged him in her excitement but before Red could react, she was pulling away again and insisting they start at once.

He smothered the urge to pull her back into his arms, and straightened up. 'Let's go, then.'

≶

'Eely,' Nonaerom said.

She was at his side at once, her pale green eyes soft with compassion. Nonaerom wanted to despise her for daring to pity him, but instead was struck by the generosity of her spirit. He gazed up into her face in puzzlement, wondering suddenly how it was that she had ever seemed ugly to him. She was any-thing but ugly.

'Angel?' she murmured.

'I … I was wondering …' he began, and then absurdly, he found himself asking, 'are you happy?'

'I am happy when I am with you,' Eely said. 'But I am sad too, because you are sad.'

Such simplicity in her words, and yet there was a wondrous clarity and honesty in them that he had never heard in any of the lovely complex speeches made in the finest salons in the Cloudlands. There, beauty was offered up as a fragmentation and shading of word and meaning, as clever implication and subtle poetic encryption. How had they come to see this as the only kind of beauty that words could aspire to? he wondered. How had they neg-lected to see that clarity and directness were beauty, too? Was it possible that the winged folk had allowed their ideal of beauty to become narrow and exclusive?

He thought of the wingstone and suddenly was

not surprised that it had found its way into Eely's hands. Attuned as it was to beauty, it had obviously seen something in her that he had been unable to see. The thought shamed him, for he was a Prince of the Cloudlands and a lover of beauty. He would not have believed it if someone had told him that he would fail to recognise beauty, but here it had stood before him and he had not seen it. And he thought no other of his people would have seen Eely any more clearly.

What did that mean? And what had changed to clear his vision?

'Do you want me to bring you some fruit?' Eely asked softly, and the gentleness in her eyes was echoed by the kindness in her fingers. Nonaerom shook his head, stunned to realise that the sight and sound of Eely was filling his senses with the same delight he had once felt in seeing a perfect sculpture or walking through a perfumed garden where the scents had been cultivated to provide an exquisite landscape of odour.

'I am broken and yet I can see beauty more clearly

now than when I was whole and beautiful myself,' he thought. 'More clearly than when I held the wingstone in my palm.'

What did that mean?

'Eely,' he murmured. 'Eely, you are beautiful.'

He had not meant to say that aloud and yet the words were true. Instead of being shocked or surprised, she only smiled unselfconsciously. 'You make me feel real,' she said. 'You came here and you saw me and you spoke to me and you made it so that other people could see me.' She was speaking so softly that he strained to hear her. 'You made me real so that I could think better and I think … I think you are making me beautiful.'

Nonaerom reeled inwardly, for surely these graceful words were not coming from the dull-witted, blushing simpleton he had permitted to serve him. The realisation of his own arrogance struck him at the same time as he recognised that she was using the word beauty in a way that he had never heard it used.

She went on. 'You came and changed all of us,

Angel. Iakas and Red, Cora and the roofies. You brought us all together and you made us talk and help one another. You made all of us beautiful like you. Beautiful inside.'

Before he could begin to utter the thoughts boiling through his mind, Eely was standing up and draping her shawl around her shoulders, saying she had better go and fetch some food before the market closed. She was gone then, leaving him feeling strangely diminished by her absence. And yet in a way he was glad to be alone, because her words were playing through his mind, seeming to reshape it. Then other words played themselves out in his memory.

The words of the red-haired guard when Nonaerom had cried that he was ugly because he was broken.

Surely beauty is not so easily broken, unless by beauty you just mean a vase or a necklace or something ...

He had never thought of it before but his people did see beauty only in things that could be touched and seen, smelled or tasted. Food or objects or music or perfume. People too, but only if they were beautiful in the same way that a vase or a statue was beautiful.

Beautiful on the outside.

He thought of Iakas's words, just before she had stormed out.

There is beauty in our world, Prince, she had said, *though maybe it is not the kind you and your people can love because it's not something you can see to worship.*

And she was right, he thought. Back in the Cloudlands, he would never have seen Eely's gentle humanity and kindness as beautiful, nor Iakas's fierce pride and independence. He would not have seen beauty in the faces of the roofies' listening rapt to his tales of the Cloudlands, or in the longing he had seen in the big guard's eyes when they rested on Iakas.

Suddenly the concept of beauty was as elusive as the wingstone and this brought the shocking thought to him that the wingstone had become elusive because the winged folk had been giving it only one kind of beauty. Maybe it had tired of it, just as a person would tire of eating the same thing over and over, no matter how delicious it was.

Nonaerom sat up, ignoring the stiffness and pain of his wings, for he had thought of something else that the red-haired rift guard had said. He had spoken of duty and he was right in pointing out that it was Nonaerom's duty to return to his own world no matter how he felt about being unable to fly. He must explain what he had discovered. They would resist the idea of extending their definition of beauty, just as he would have done before coming to Quentaris. But the winged folk must be made to listen for if they did not, the Cloudlands and Landfall City alike would fail and both the winged and wingless perish. The wingstone had appeared in time to bestow its power on a ship containing the last of two races from a destroyed world. They had landed helplessly on a cold, inhospitable planet and the wingstone had saved them. But if they could not find a way to content the stone, then the civilisation that they had built on their adopted world would fall.

Must be falling even now, he realised with a renewed sense of urgency. But as he began to rise, it came to him that even if he returned, and managed, crippled and humbled, to convince them that they must change their attitudes, what use would there be when he had not the wingstone they needed to survive?

'It must be found,' Nonaerom murmured.

≋

'I don't understand,' Iakas said. 'It's not working.'

It was dawn and they had spent the night moving through Quentaris. The Orphans' Hospital had been their last stop and they had both thought this would be where the wingstone would be found. But when they had bid the healers farewell at last, they had still been empty-handed. Red supposed that he looked as washed out as Iakas, though she showed no signs of being ready to give up. He could not help but admire her persistence, though he was beginning to wonder if they had been wrong after all.

'We haven't tried the Studio yet,' he said wearily. 'The first ferry leaves at sunup ...' He wondered what Cora would have to say when he didn't make it to the briefing.

'No,' Iakas said glumly. 'If it wasn't in the Cathedral or the songhouse or the hospital, it won't be there. There's something else we haven't figured out.' She looked at Red. 'What other sorts of beauty are there? Something they wouldn't have in the Cloudlands.'

He did not utter the words pressing at his lips. This was not the moment to talk of the beauty of love, even if she were receptive, and there was no certainty in that. 'It sounds like there wouldn't be too much humility in the Cloudlands, or gentleness or kindness because they all sound so intense and fierce and proud.'

'Yes, that's the sort of thing I mean. Now where would we find a place where people feel gentle or kind in Quentaris?'

'I would have thought the hospital, but they're all busy healing people and diseases. Kindness ...' Red murmured. All at once, he found himself remembering how happy Eely had looked when she had come out of the Paupers' market the day he had seen Iakas jump. Hadn't she talked about how friendly and kind people were, singing and telling stories as they worked. He looked at Iakas. 'I know where we'll find the wingstone!' he said triumphantly, and he caught hold of her hand and dragged her after him.

≈

In half an hour, they were speaking to an enormous woman with alarming red hair and beautiful grey eyes who had introduced herself as Ma Coglin.

'Beauty?' the old woman laughed, three chins wobbling as she gestured about the dank-smelling market where women and a few men wearing grey aprons were scrubbing floors or tables. Others bustled industriously this way and that carrying buckets or bags. 'As you see, we don't worry too much about trappings here. All the money we get goes into feeding people and buying blankets and medicines and so on. People donate things but there is a never ending stream of needy visitors here, and not all of them have something to trade. But no one ever goes away from the Paupers' market hungry or wet or cold.'

'So, people are unusually happy here?' Iakas asked eagerly.

The big woman tilted her an enigmatic look. 'Happiness. Well now, you're young.' She looked at Red. 'You too, lad, for all you're built like half a house. So both of you probably think that the purpose of life is to find happiness. Most of the people who come here feel like they got cheated out of their share of it. But I'm an old woman and I've seen a lot since I go through life with my eyes open. And what I see is that happiness ain't a destination or a thing you get to keep for good. It comes in rough little clumps that you don't see until you stumble over them, and maybe you don't see them even then. You can't find them by working or saving or even by wanting them. They come or don't, like rain or sunshine.'

'But ... then what do *you* think is the purpose of life?' Iakas asked, distracted from their quest by this strange, compelling woman.

Ma Coglin gave another great bellow of laughter. 'The gods know, maybe. Mostly I'm too busy to wonder, but since you ask, I think the purpose of life is to live and to help other folk along when you can. It doesn't much matter what you do other than that, except you might as well do whatever it is you decide to do with guts and passion. Unless you are a complete dunderhead, and there are plenty of them around, you will find your own clumps of happiness as you go along. But most of life is struggle and strife and muddle and a wearisome lot of silliness. What were your names again?' she asked suddenly.

Red told her because Iakas was looking as if someone had given her a knock on the head.

'Red and Iakas,' Ma Coglan said, as if she was filing them away somewhere. 'Well now, what exactly was it you wanted since neither of you looks hungry in the way that food or blankets will satisfy.'

'We … we wondered if you'd mind us looking around a bit,' Red temporised. 'We are looking for something that a friend might have dropped here.'

Ma Coglin squinted her eyes at him. 'And what friend would that be?'

'Her name is Eely,' Iakas said. 'She's about my height but …'

'Eely,' Ma Coglan said, and her smile widened.

'That child is something special, ain't she? When she visits it's like a piece of sunshine got in here. But I didn't see her drop anything just now ...'

'She was just here?' Iakas asked before Red could stop her.

Ma frowned at her. 'Course she was. Buying fruit and bread for that winged man you roofies got up there. Didn't she send you back here just now to find whatever it was that she lost?'

'She didn't exactly lose anything,' Red said, ignoring the look Iakas shot at him. 'Do you have a little time, because maybe we need to explain this to you?'

Ma Coglin lifted her brows and beamed at him rakishly. 'We're between shifts and I've always got time for a good story, boy.'

≥

'So, you think this wingstone is here?' Ma asked. 'Why?'

'Because of how Eely looked that time Red bumped into her,' Iakas said. Red had told her on

their way to the Paupers' market about the acciden-
tal meeting in the street.

'Because she looked happy?'

'She told me that this was a wonderful place
where people sang while they worked. She said they
were kind to one another and laughed a lot. But I've
never heard anyone say such things about the
Paupers' market before.'

'It is true that everyone is in good spirits lately,'
Ma said thoughtfully. 'But ... you think this wingstone is causing it? That it's exerting some magical
influence?'

'I don't know whether it is magic, but if it were
here and if it acts the way Nonaerom said, well, it
could explain why the atmosphere changed,' Red said.

Ma Coglin shrugged. 'You can look about as you
like, touch whatever you want. But don't take too
long because people will begin arriving soon to set
up the night stalls.'

Red nodded and rose. 'Thank you for the time.'

The older woman grinned. 'It has been interest-
ing, but let me tell you that Eely is happy here
because she feels like she can help. She does help.

She works hard but more importantly, she is kind and sweet and she listens to people that no one else will even look at. There is no magical stone. People smile and laugh and tell her stories because Eely is the way she is. That's all.'

She bustled away leaving Iakas and Red looking around helplessly.

'Eely said it's small,' Red murmured.

'Let's just go around touching everything,' Iakas said, finally.

❧

'I don't understand,' Red muttered at last, his voice almost lost in the din of arriving stallholders setting up for a night's trade. There were urchins arriving, shouting obscenities and ducking when Ma Coglin boxed their ears for their language, and a group of the half starved gnomes that had come through a rift a few months past filed in looking less desperate, and talking about mines in another city.

'It must be somewhere else,' Iakas said. 'The beauty of knowledge maybe? The library or the university?' She was so tired that she was beginning to see things.

'No,' Red said. 'It's here, or it was here. You didn't see Eely that day.'

Iakas sighed. 'Let's go back and talk to Nonaerom.'

An
End and
a Beginning

Nonaerom woke to the sound of a commotion outside the roost. He could hear Iakas's voice and the soft, beautifully modulated voice of the roofie, Arrow. He could not tell what they were saying, though he thought there was anger in both voices.

Arrow had visited him several times to begin with, and despite the smoothness of his manners and his undeniably fair face and limbs, not to mention the honed perfection of his words, Nonaerom did not like him.

Now he wondered if it was because Arrow's beauty was merely the sort of beauty that he had been trained to revere, rather than the deeper beauty which he had come to see in Eely. Having seen that inner beauty, which transcended its own outer form, he was unable to be moved by Arrow.

The flap was flung open and Iakas entered, her eyes snapping with anger. 'Really, he is too much. He can't order me to leave the roof.'

'Is it true that you are breaking roofie taboos in having me up here?' Red asked softly.

'If I am, it is a stupid rule and it's time someone disobeyed it,' Iakas snapped. Then she caught sight of Nonaerom sitting up in his bed, and her own expression changed. 'Nonaerom … what is it? You look …'

'I do not know how I look,' Nonaerom said. 'But I do know that it is less important than how I feel. I did not know that before and so I misled you. I sent you to look for the wingstone where there was beauty and because I spoke of beauty in a certain way, you looked only for a certain kind of beauty. That is why you could not find it. Because the wingstone has been drawn to a different, deeper sort of beauty. The sort you cannot see with your eyes but with your heart and soul. The sort of beauty that Eely has taught me to see.'

'Eely!' Iakas said.

'Nonaerom, we had the same thought,' Red broke in. 'But we spent the night searching in places where there were different kinds of beauty. We thought we had it figured out a couple of hours ago because I remembered seeing Eely in the street one day, looking so happy because she had come from a wonderful place. I thought that must be where she had dropped the wingstone, but we went there and searched the place from top to bottom. We didn't find anything. The woman who runs the Paupers' market — that's what it is called — said it wasn't a stone making people happy. It was Eely, because she is kind and sweet and generous.'

'Eely *is* all of those things,' Nonaerom said softly. 'I thought it was a dream but when I woke in the rift cave I saw a wondrously lovely maiden bending over me. When that maiden could not be found, I thought I had imagined it, but I was right. It was Eely that I saw truly and deeply in that moment. I have been too blind to realise it until now. It does not surprise me that the wingstone went to her. The only wonder is that it left her.'

He stopped and all three of them saw their own thought form on the face of the other two.

In that moment Eely pushed through the flap to the roost awkwardly, her arms full. 'I went by home to get …'

'Eely.' Red stepped towards her and took her bag and parcels, setting them down on the ground.

'What is the matter?' she asked, becoming aware of the tension in the roost. 'Is something wrong?'

'Nothing is wrong,' Red said, taking her hands in his and noticing again how pretty she had grown, how bright her eyes were. 'Eely, do you remember a while back when I asked you about the wingstone?'

Eely nodded.

'You remember how you put it into your pocket and when you looked, you couldn't find it? It had fallen out, you thought. Well, we have been thinking that maybe it didn't fall out at all. Maybe it's still in your pocket.'

Eely instinctively dug into the pockets of her vest, then she opened her hands to display the collection of objects she carried. There was no wingstone.

Red sighed with disappointment. 'I thought for certain that it ...'

'Wait!' Iakas said softly. She looked at Nonaerom. 'You said that it reflects whatever it is with, whatever it was attracted to, right?'

He nodded.

'And remember how the soothsayer said it had found its truest form? Well, let's say Red was right and it stayed with Eely, then it would make itself into something like her, wouldn't it? In which case it wouldn't look like the wingstone and it wouldn't seem to be beautiful at first sight. It might even look ... ugly.' She gave Eely an apologetic look.

'That is true,' Nonaerom said, sounding breath-
less with hope. 'Please, my dear Eely, will you let me
see what you have there?'

In answer, she offered the contents of her pockets:
a few stones, a shell, a twist of paper, a comb, a nut.
It was the latter that Nonaerom reached out to touch
and the nut began to glow brightly at once. When it
faded, there lay the wingstone, a perfect feather in
transparent miniature.

'Oh,' Eely said in surprise.

'A nut!' Red said, half laughing in disbelief.

'Exactly,' Iakas said. 'Something hidden inside
something else.' She smiled at Eely. 'That's you.'

Eely smiled, but there was sadness in her eyes as
she picked up the wingstone and held it out to
Nonaerom. He shook his head. 'It chose you, Eely.
And you are its rightful Holder now. It would not
have remained with you in this guise unless it was
very certain of where it wanted to be. It had a thousand chances to return to me and it did not do so.'

'But … you have to take it back to your world,
you said,' Iakas protested.

Nonaerom nodded gravely. 'It must be returned to our world for my people cannot survive without it. But …' he turned to Eely. 'I am wondering if you would consider coming back with me. I know that your sister and your friends are here, and this is your world, but my world is lovely too and if there is now to be traverse between this world and mine, perhaps you can return here for visits.'

'How can you ask her to come with you?' Iakas demanded. 'How would it be for her in a world where people want everything to be beautiful and perfect?'

Nonaerom made his answer directly to Eely.

'Eely, you asked me once how breaking something beautiful could make it ugly. The answer is that beauty can't be broken. You knew that and I didn't. But I know something else now. A deeper truth. Sometimes breaking a thing can make it better. Having my wing broken has made me able to see what I could not see before. It is true that when we first go to my world, both of us will be regarded as ugly. But they will learn the truth because if they cannot change the way they see things, our world will not survive. Give me a chance, Eely, and I will teach them to see the beauty in you, just as I have learned to see it.'

Eely looked down at the wingstone and her face changed, the confusion becoming a blossoming of wonder. Then she opened her hand out and they all saw that the wingstone had become a nut again.

'You see,' Nonaerom said softly. 'The wingstone has chosen you as its Holder, Eely, and on my world, it is said that *whoever Holds the wingstone, Holds the world.*'

Red stepped forward. 'Look, this is not fair. You are asking her to go to a world where there is danger and violence, and why should she, just because you have a use for her?'

'Because I want to be of use,' Eely spoke softly and firmly. 'I have never really been needed here. You've been kind to me, Red, and Cora has always taken care of me, but neither of you need me. Ma Coglin always says we should help where we can and I … I want to help Prince Nonaerom.'

They all noticed that it was the first time she had not called him Angel.

'Well,' Red said. 'I wonder what Cora will say.'

⇛

'I don't like this one bit,' Cora muttered.

'Hush,' Red said. 'Eely has made her decision and we must respect it if we care for her.'

'That's just it,' Cora sighed. 'I have grown so used to making her decisions and doing all the deciding. I thought I was weary of it and that Eely was a burden I could not escape, but now she is going away ...' She stopped and he caught the glitter of tears in her eyes. 'Somehow I never noticed how much I care for her and how sweet she is. I'm like that stupid winged man not seeing how lovely she is.'

'She'll visit once the diplomats sort out all of the trade treaties,' Red said, but he had to blink hard to keep his own eyes clear.

'It will be more than a few years before that happens,' Cora muttered. 'You know how it works.

One step forward and ten back, and it sounds like there are plenty of internal problems to settle before they can even think of setting up links with Quentaris. And double that time length if they turn out to be prickly and difficult.'

'You can accept your promotion now, and Eely is happy,' Red pointed out.

Cora gave a teary laugh. 'I'm glad she's happy, but somehow that promotion seems less of a gain if it means I have to lose Eely.'

The sound of marching feet drew their attention and they both turned to see Iakas coming along the street with several of the roofies. Red saw this with a surprising thrust of triumph at the knowledge that Iakas must be gaining ground in her attempt to win the roofies away from Arrow's influence. But rather than looking happy, she looked fierce and wan at the same time as she stopped before Nonaerom.

'You'd better take good care of Eely or you'll have the roofies to answer to,' she said.

Nonaerom did not smile or sneer or bridle. He only reached out and lay an enormous hand on her shoulder. 'You have my word upon it, Iakas, but you do not need it for Eely is precious to me, and soon she will be precious to winged and land walkers alike in my world.'

Iakas nodded, thinking that the winged man looked older and more weary than he had done before, but more beautiful as well. To her surprise and confusion, he put his arms around her and embraced her gently as she had often longed for him to do. But when he released her, she released him, telling herself that angels were not for ordinary people, no matter how well they could jump. She hugged Eely goodbye and wished her luck and Red did the same. Last of all, Cora went to Eely and the sisters held one another tightly for a long time before kissing and parting. Cora spoke sternly to Nonaerom, who listened gravely and then nodded.

Rad de La'rel approached then, to speak with Nonaerom and Eely. The young guide had spent most of the previous evening with Nonaerom, asking questions, drawing maps and making calculations until he was sure he knew where the entrance to

Nonaerom's world was. Now he would guide them to the rift that would send them home and at the same time, he would take readings so that the crossing pattern could be sought again.

Nonaerom spoke one last time before he turned away. 'You have healed my body and you have opened my eyes, my Quentaran friends. For that, I thank you. Goodbye.' He held out his hand to Eely, and when she set her own hand shyly in his enormous grasp Nonaerom led her after Rad, limping slightly because of the dragging weight of his damaged wing. The three vanished into the darkness of the rift caves, and after a short time, the roofies drifted away. Cora stayed a little longer, but then she went back to the guardhouse, head bowed, leaving Iakas and Red standing side by side at the rift wall.

~

'So, that's that,' Red said softly.

'I feel all emptied out,' Iakas murmured. Then without warning, she burst into a storm of tears.

After a stunned moment, Red slid an arm around her shoulders.

'He would have taken you too, if you had asked.'

Iakas glared at him through her tears. 'Are you mad? I don't want to go to Nonaerom's world. I belong here.'

'I'm glad to hear that,' Red said.

'You are? Why?' Iakas asked.

Red shrugged and gave her a lop-sided grin. 'Because then you'd be crying for days on end instead of properly getting to the job of turning the roofies into an order. Which Cora thinks is a brilliant idea by the way. She told me to let you know that she would stand as one of the sponsors. If you wait a few weeks until she is captain, her word will carry quite a bit of weight.' Then he said casually, 'Actually, I thought for a while there that you were in love with Eely's angel.'

Iakas dabbed her eyes in silence, then she said in a low thoughtful voice, 'When I looked at him, something in me felt light and unbearably bright. I longed to be special to him and I wanted him to desire me. I dreamed of flying with him and how it would be. But he belongs somewhere else and maybe my feet are planted too firmly on the ground for me to love a winged man.'

'The ground? Not on a roof?' Red echoed.

Iakas looked at him, because there was a peculiar catch in his voice. For once, he didn't smile and even as she realised how much she liked his smile, something inside her fluttered as if it wanted to take flight.

She took a deep breath, thinking that Nonaerom was not the only one who could learn to see differently. But she said, 'Let's just say that I wouldn't love anyone who could get away from me so easily.'

Red gave a startled laugh and watched her walk jauntily away.

THE QUENTARIS CHRONICLES

Swords of Quentaris

Paul Collins

Rad de La'rel is a street urchin who yearns to be a guide to adventurers in the rift caves of Quentaris. But before he can claim his birthright, he must escape the Thieves' Guild and the notorious Vindon Nibhelline with the help of his friend Tulcia. Only then will he be proclaimed the greatest guide since his ancestor, the legendary Nathine de La'rel.

Paul Collins has been short-listed for many Australian science fiction and fantasy awards. He has won the Aurealis, the William Atheling, and the inaugural Peter McNamara Awards. His books include *The Great Ferret Race, The Dog King, Dragonlinks, Slaves of Quentaris* and *Dragonlords of Quentaris*.

ISBN 0 7344 0470 0

Quentaris in Flames

Michael Pryor

When a fire is deliberately lit in the city of Quentaris, Nisha Fairsight and her minstrel friend Tal investigate and soon uncover a plot threatening its inhabitants. Adding to the city's woes is the threat of invasion from the vicious, insect-like Zolka, who are making it even more dangerous than usual to pass through the rift caves.

Nisha must discover her fire-magic heritage and her place in Quentaris. Will she be able to save the city and her friends?

Michael Pryor is the author of many popular and award-winning novels and short stories, including *Beneath Quentaris* and *Stones of Quentaris*. Michael lives in Melbourne with his wife Wendy and two daughters, Celeste and Ruby.

ISBN 0 7344 0469 7

The Perfect Princess

Jenny Pausacker

Tab Vidler is an orphan who works for the Dung Brigade, sweeping the streets of Quentaris. One day she meets a mysterious stranger called Azt Marossa and before long she is helping him escape from the Archon's guards and avoid Duelph and Nibhelline sword fighters. Most importantly of all, she's finding out what really happened to her heroine, the Perfect Princess, who fled Quentaris years ago …

Jenny Pausacker has written sixty books for young people, from picture books and junior fantasies to science fiction and young adult novels, winning several awards. Jenny's titles include *Scam*, *Looking for Blondie* and *Death by Water* (Crime Waves), and *The Rings* in Lothian's After Dark series.

ISBN 0 7344 0586 3

The Revognase

Lucy Sussex

Life in the city of Quentaris is never dull. The city's two feuding families, the Blues and the Greens, have just held a battle in the market. There has been a duel between wizards and a burglary at the Villains' Guild. And the Chief Soothsayer has just prophesied another disaster: 'I see a disc of changing colours, passing from hand to hand. I see murder, misery and mayhem. I see the disc destroying everyone who touches it!'

Lucy Sussex has been published internationally and in various genres, including children's fiction, literary criticism, horror and crime fiction. She has won the Ditmar and Aurealis Awards, and been short-listed for the Kelly Awards (for crime writing) and the Wilderness Society Environment Award for children's literature.

ISBN 0 7344 0495 6

Beneath Quentaris

Michael Pryor

In the fabled city of magic, mystery and mayhem, young Nisha is struggling to come to terms with her fire-magician heritage. With the help of young minstrel Tal, Nisha learns to control her power while being swept up in events that threaten Quentaris itself, leading her to the fabulous and forbidding underground streets of Lower Quentaris.

ISBN 0 7344 0556 1

Slaves of Quentaris

Paul Collins

Yukin and his mate, Yulen, flee their campsite when Akcarum slave-traders attack. Unable to escape the Akcarum hunter birds, they are caught and transported to Quentaris. On their journey through the rift caves Yukin discovers a power that taps into the senses of insects and animals. But can it save them in time?

ISBN 0 7344 0557 X

Stones of Quentaris

Michael Pryor

Who is stealing the stones of Quentaris? With Quentaris preparing for the annual Carnivale celebration, Jaq Coblin is thrown into an adventure with four mysterious strangers, powerful magic and a horde of barbarians made of sand. What can Jaq do but use his wits and hold on tight?

ISBN 0 7344 0619 3

Dragonlords of Quentaris

Paul Collins

Rad de La'rel is about to sign a trade agreement with the devious Fendonians when he is captured by sky pirates. Sold into slavery, he becomes a pawn to the all-conquering drag-onlords of Udari. When he returns to Quentaris it has been invaded by the very creatures Rad has escaped from. Worse — nearly every citizen is wearing a slave's neck collar.

Can the famous Quentaran rift guide release his people from the grip of the invaders?

ISBN 0 7344 0620 7

The Ancient Hero

Sean McMullen

An ancient stalker prowls Quentaris. He seeks to destroy a powerful book of spells, but must get past the Murderers' Guild, the City Watch, and the City Militia. No one is safe, or so it seems, until a student called Zelder translates the spell that could be the key to his undoing …

Sean McMullen is the acclaimed author of numerous science fiction and fantasy books. He has won a dozen awards, and his work has been translated into eight languages. Sean is currently studying medieval literature at Melbourne University, and is a member of its karate and fencing clubs.

ISBN 0 7344 0657 6

Treasure Hunters of Quentaris

Margo Lanagan

Tikko wants to delay growing up and becoming a rift guide, and Lord Eustachio Doro is unsure of following in the footsteps of his family. When they are thrown together to become the latest treasure hunters in the rift caves found in the mountains near Quentaris, they are less concerned with their futures and more interested in finding their fortunes.

Margo Lanagan is an award-winning author whose books have been shortlisted for the New South Wales Premier's and Aurealis Awards; she also won the best young adult short story in the 2000 Aurealis Awards for *The Queen's Notice*. *Treasure Hunters of Quentaris* is Margo's first book published by Lothian.

ISBN 0 7344 0690 8

The Mind Master

John Heffernan

Torrad, a young boy working for the Miragho family, possesses strange magical powers of the mind. Through his ability, he has uncovered an evil plot against the people of Quentaris. But can one boy change the course of Quentaran history?

John Heffernan is the author of numerous acclaimed publications including *Spud, Rachael's Forrest, More Than Gold, My Dog* (CBC Book of the Year for Younger Readers and CBC Honour Book in 2002) and *Two Summers*. Formerly a lecturer with several university degrees, including a Masters in Educational Psychology, he has opted out of the academic life in preference to running a sheep and cattle property with his wife in Northern New South Wales.

ISBN 0 7344 0656 8